IT AIN'T ALL JOKES!

LAWAN A. TAYLOR THOMPSON

LaWan A. Taylor Thompson

Copyright © 2020 by LaWan A. Taylor Thompson

All rights reserved.

Published and Printed in the United States of America

ISBN 9798620777846

Book design by Ashlaine Designs, LLC – Raleigh, NC

Second Edition

LaWan A. Taylor Thompson

It Ain't All Jokes!

DEDICATION

This book is dedicated to all mankind that grew up without a good mother in your life. You may have felt abandoned, alone, you may have been abused and misunderstood. Whatever the case may have been and whatever emotions overwhelmed you, be encouraged knowing you survived. Remember; you are an overcomer. You are more than a conqueror. You are fearfully and wonderfully made. You are wise. You are favored. You are blessed.

I dedicate this book to my amazing father, Michael George Taylor. Raising me as a single dad I'm sure was not easy, but you did it. You loved me unconditionally and you loved me through it all. Lastly, I also dedicate this book to my sister, Teara "Tia" Washington. We've been through a lot, endured a lot together and apart, yet we made it through. God has been exceptionally wonderful and what the devil meant for evil, God worked it out for our good.

.

LaWan A. Taylor Thompson

LaWan A. Taylor Thompson

CONTENTS

1 Acknowledgements

1	Introduction…LaWan	V
2	In The Beginning	1
3	Growing Up Wanda	5
4	If God Never Saved Me…	
	My Daddy Was More Than Enough!	43
5	Chronicles of Wanda	53
6	The Late 80's…Oh My!	61
7	Satan's Cousin…My Ex-husband!	99
8	Peace, Blessings, Restoration…	134
9	The Journey Continues…	149
10	Discussion Questions…	155

It Ain't All Jokes!

ACKNOWLEDGMENTS

I want to first give thanks and praise to my Lord & Savior Jesus Christ. Without Him, I literally would not have been able to accomplish such a project as writing this book. It was HARD. There were tears, moments of pain, an inkling or two of regret, and just as shame tried to creep in again, I had to remember a sermon I preached titled, "I was caught, but now I'm free!" *For whom the son has set free is free indeed*! Hallelujah!

I want to secondly thank a few friends! Minister Darlene Brown Garrett, I love you for always loving me. For YEARS you would say to me, "LaWan, when are you writing your book called The Chronicles of Wanda?" Lol I would laugh heartedly not thinking that I ever would. As my manicurist, you were easy to talk to, and most of the stuff I shared made you laugh. Such a great sounding board you were without judgment. You have been a friend from beginning to end. And the best is still yet to come.

Pastor Joseph Brown my true friend for life! (I'm literally tearing up) You have poured into me since the day we met in 1993. I was 9 months pregnant with my youngest son Kent, sitting in Greater Mt. Calvary Holy

LaWan A. Taylor Thompson

Church. It was a Friday night and Pastor James Sturdivant was preaching. I was in labor and refused to leave before benediction. LOL You said to me with a warm smile, "I don't know who you are young lady, but you are a beautiful and bold woman, and I see so much of what God is going to do in you." After I thanked you and we hugged, you said, "I'm Deacon Joe Brown, now get yourself to that hospital." I laughed and said, "I'm LaWan Hight and this is baby number 4, I'm good, I got this." LOL God immediately knitted us together and I cannot imagine life without you in it. I love you and I thank you for loving me unconditionally and for NEVER giving up on me.

Amy Nichelle Langley....GIRLLLLAHHH! Lol See, I can type the way we talk! LOL Your life has blessed my life. Just when I wanted to just write my book and keep it as a personal journal, YOUR published book, *In Search of Amy* pushed my book to life! I appreciate you so very much! I thank God you are that friend who is not afraid to step out on faith and believe God no matter what. Watching your faith activated pushed my faith to higher levels. God told me one day, "Amy loves you and she has your best interest at heart. You can trust her because she is the true definition of a Sister's Keeper!" (oh boy, I'm crying again) I love you, girlie!!

To my kind-hearted, smart, crafty, witty, resilient, charming, strong, and talented children, Courtney,

It Ain't All Jokes!

Kendall, Kenard, and Kent. I love you more than life itself. God saw fit to bless me with you. It wasn't easy raising four growing children alone, but I made it, and thanks be to God I don't look like what I've been through. God never put more or me than I was able to bear. He was my strength through it all. Thank you for loving your mother (me) with all that you have. I wasn't perfect and I tried to raise you as best as I could without a biological example of what a loving mother should look like. Every mistake I've made, please forgive me. Every gift you didn't receive for Christmas, please forgive me. Every material item that I couldn't buy for you, please forgive me. For every unfair spanking, please forgive me. I hope this book will help you understand me a little better.

    To my amazing, super intelligent, beautiful, successful and educated Editor, my gifted daughter, Courtney LaWan Taylor! Thank you for taking the time to skillfully edit my first book with such honesty and catching what I felt would be the best sentence. Lol I am so very proud of the woman you've become. A college graduate with two degrees, author, educator, chef, and one that I gleam from. You are the epitome of a true blessing from God. I am not only HAPPY that you are my editor, but I'm APPRECIATIVE to have a supportive daughter like you.

LaWan A. Taylor Thompson

Lastly, but certainly not least, I want to thank my remarkable husband, Kevin Thompson! You are the ultimate supporter, provider, listener, voice of reason, lover, friend and the absolute BEST husband that any woman could ever ask God for. Honestly, I never wanted to remarry. When we met, I made that perfectly clear on our second date when you professed your love for me. I remember thinking, *"wow, this guy is whipped already,"* Lol but maturity said, "No, this man knows what he wants for his life!" I appreciate your patience! I'm the first to admit, I'm not the easiest person to love, let alone like. But you saw in me what God showed you that I was ordained to be your wife. You married the healed, restored, renewed, revived, amazingly strong, forgiving, loving…Yep, you married the BEST parts of me! Husband, I love you with everything in me! Often, I say to you, I don't deserve a man like you. But God corrected me one day and said, "yes, you do." Being married to you has reignited my faith in the institution of marriage! I appreciate you and thank God for you. And I believe what God has joined together nothing shall tear us apart.

INTRODUCTION... LAWAN

I am LaWan Alexis Taylor Thompson. I am proud to say that I'm a wife, mother, grandmother, Christian Comedienne, Event Host, Caretaker of my father, Zumba Instructor, Entrepreneur, Intercessor, Mentor, Minister. I'm beyond blessed to be alive. I am an abuse survivor and a Thyroid cancer survivor. Although I've been diagnosed with Arthritis, I believe God for the manifestation of total healing. Through this journey I found my purpose and passion. Although I've walked through the valley of the shadow of death, I came through unburned, rebirthed, wiser, restored, uplifted, and stronger than ever before. I dare say, I don't look like what I've been through. My accomplishments are greater than my challenges and still God is adding so much favor and flavor to my existence. I am an overcomer with the courage to be all that God has created in me to be.

God is so amazingly wonderful, and I never would've thought in the beginning that I'd be at this place. My failures turned into faith! My stress turned into shouts! My gloom turned into glory! My negatives turned into positives! My frowns turned into smiles! My weeping turned into joy! My anger turned into happiness! My unforgiveness turned into love!

LaWan A. Taylor Thompson

But before I became any of that, this is my story...

LaWan A. Taylor Thompson

IN THE BEGINNING

Born and raised in Washington, DC, February 26th, in the early 70's, it was a snowy and very cold winter morning from what I was told. Born to the parents of Wanda Cecelia Sutton and Michael George Taylor, I was their first child. My parents never married and from what I've learned, their relationship ended when I turned around two years old. Both of my parents graduated from Cardozo Senior High School, while my Daddy furthered his education by attending the University of Maryland, my mom became a Secretary at NIH (National Institute of Health) in Bethesda, Maryland. They were both from the Northwest quadrant of, Washington, D.C., affectionately known by native Washingtonians as *Uptown*.

Both of my parents were extroverts. How those two extroverts managed to meet, date, and conceive a child is beyond me. But I guess opposites do attract because they were polar opposites in every sense of the word. My mother was born to Margaret Sutton and Dennis (I never knew his last name). She had three sisters and one

It Ain't All Jokes!

brother; however, she was Margaret & Dennis' only child together. She was the kind of woman that lived dangerously. She was strong-willed, stubborn, rebellious, and embraced the lawless side of life. If the adventure was crazy enough to almost lose your life accomplishing it, my mother was all in. My mother was a brown skinned African American woman, very pretty, shapely, with a head full of soft, beautiful, healthy hair. On the rare occasions that she would smile, it was a pretty one. A mouth full of semi-white teeth. I don't remember her laugh because she didn't find much funny. Always serious, mean, and evil acting most of the times, I didn't think she possessed the ability to actually laugh. Although Eddie Murphy was one of her favorite comedians, she would chuckle just a little at his jokes with a slight smirk and say "that Eddie Murphy is the funniest nigga in Hollywood." I found her definition of funny to be out of the ordinary because she didn't laugh out loud. My mother was a chain cigarette smoker. *Kool* was her brand of choice. She drank beer occasionally but didn't drink wine or other forms of liquor; unfortunately my mother was a drug addict. She was addicted to heroin; an intravenous drug abuser. She didn't have many friends. Never really got along with people for too long especially other women. The bulk of her friends were drug addicts as well, so their relationships were extremely toxic. As the saying goes, *birds of a feather flock together.* My mother was married. She married twice actually and both men were the epitome of loser. Her first husband, Guy, died of a drug overdose in 1981. Her second husband, Petey, is still alive and he isn't doing well physically. Drug usage has caused him to live with an incurable disease. My mother had two children, my sister Tia and I. Although she was legally married, neither husband was an instrument in raising us. Neither men were our fathers. They were deadbeat husbands and stepfathers who were selfish, felons, thieves, weirdos and strung out drug addicts. Such bad examples of what black men should aspire to be.

My Daddy is a kind, meek, strong man who love people and everybody loved him. *"Black Mike"* or *"Troop"* is what his friends and family affectionately nicknamed him. He is the eldest son of Pauline Taylor and she only birthed two boys. He has no biological sisters but gained many female friends who they've bonded tightly and he calls them his sisters and I affectionately call them my aunts and love them just the same. He was the fun father who loved me unconditionally. My Daddy spoiled me rotten! Lol People would tell him to "stop spoiling LaWan," but he listened as their words fell on deaf ears at the same time. Daddy has a total of three children and he married his youngest son's mom. I'm the eldest and the only girl. Dad was a handsome, dark skinned African American man, slender build, roughly five feet eight inches tall, with big brown eyes, and a pearly white smile. As he's gotten older, he's still a handsome, distinguished senior citizen. One of the smartest men I know, loves to read, and research history. Dad was a dancing machine! He loved going to parties and will make any DJ feel proud. Lol Daddy was educated through DC Public Schools. After completing necessary studies at University of Maryland, he was hired as an Assistant Teacher at Marie H. Reed Community Learning Center in Washington, D.C. Daddy was almost my third-grade teacher, but the principal knew enough than to allow me to be a student in Dad's class. Dad has always been drug and alcohol free. He ran marathons, ate healthy mostly, exercised daily, and lived his life to the fullest. He's never been arrested and was a stickler for obeying the laws of the land. Dad was a leader in the community, mentoring many young people especially the young African American males as their basketball coach. Dad was always encouraging, motivating, easy to talk too, and easy to love. Non-judgmental, constantly seeing the best in people, Dad is an extremely positive person and a giver; continually putting the needs of others before his own. God blessed him with a compassionate heart.

GROWING UP WANDA

As long as I can remember I never loved my mother. Honestly, I hated her with every fiber in my being! She was a very mean, scary, evil, abusive, angry, manipulating, hateful, uncompassionate, uncaring, unloving, and a non-supportive mother, who put her drug addiction before the needs of her children. My mother was truly used by the Devil. I don't believe she purposely had children just to abuse and harm them. She had to have been possessed with an evil spirit that was greater than she was. Instead of seeking help, prayer, or even rehabilitation, she continued to allow the Devil to use her in a way that ultimately caused her to lose her life. If my Daddy didn't love me the way he did and demonstrated unconditional love, my mother's behavior and actions were a strong indication that she didn't like or love me at no given time. I managed to tell my Daddy all the time how much I hated my mother and he would pretty much respond in a positive manner saying,

"LaWan, you've got to love your mother. She's sick and she needs help and prayer."

It Ain't All Jokes!

I felt he was ridiculous for even saying some foolishness like that. The woman was hateful, and I hated her, period!

My Daddy would also say, "LaWan, promise me you'll never tell your mother that you don't love her."

I would always respond, "I promise Daddy," and I kept my word.

My sister is 4½ years younger than me and I was always responsible for her growing up. "Watch Tia," is what my mother said all the time and I hated it. I hated having a sister, and I detested having been made to babysit her. Babysitting her caused me not to always treat her kindly. I wanted to play with my friends without having an adult responsibility. Watching my sister should've been given to a responsible adult or even a teenager, not a big sister who wasn't even reliable enough to care for herself. Being that I didn't want to *"keep an eye" on* my sister, I treated her mean most times. She always admired and honored me, but I didn't appreciate nor treasure any of those moments. My mother certainly didn't set an example of what love or admiration should look like in our home or outside. She wasn't close with her three sisters or brother. They didn't get along at all. The family was extremely dysfunctional. For the most part, I was beat and cussed out almost daily by my mother. It seemed she did everything she could to tear down my self-esteem and to devalue me at such a young age. I look exactly like my Daddy. Pretty brown skin, beautiful smile with huge brown eyes.

If someone would pay me a compliment and say, "LaWan, you are so pretty!"

My mother would say, "Don't tell her that shit before it goes to her head."

Thank God my Daddy told me I was pretty and complimented me every chance he got, he protected my self-esteem unbeknownst to me. My mother wasn't the kind of mother who gave hugs or told her children that she loved them. I never received a hug from her, not once. I heard her say she loved me twice! TWICE! Both times she was high from shooting heroin in her veins. Once when I was ten years old and the last time was roughly a week before my seventeenth birthday.

My mother, sister and I lived in a filthy one-bedroom apartment. It reeked of dirty carpet, cigarette odor, dirty dishes, trash, and something sour who knows. The apartment stank! Dishes were piled up, the refrigerator, freezer and cabinets were bare, except for ice trays, a half empty RC soda, and a box of baking soda. My mother was in the bedroom with her first husband Guy. The bedroom door was shut, which I knew they were in there shooting dope in each other's veins. Many times, I've walked in the room and witnessed them and her friends shooting up, so I knew when the door was closed, my sister and I were not allowed to enter, and we better not interrupt her. She came out of the room and asked us if we were hungry. Of course, we were, woman! The last meal we had was DC Public School's lunch and that was nasty, so yes, we were starving in our childlike minds. If you aren't familiar with the effects of the drug heroin, it's a downer. Triggering the addict to function at an abnormally slow stride.

    My mother's speech was slurred as she said almost in slow motion,
    "Wan and Tia?" I remember Tia excitedly responding "Yes, Mommy!"
    I rolled my eyes. I hated my mother! I never smiled around my mother and I was always mean, mad, sarcastic and ready to go any place where she was not.
    Obviously, she didn't hear me respond, so she added a little base to her tone and said, "Hey LaWan?"
    "What," I responded in my signature curt tone. I had the world's worst attitude problem.
    She started gradually coming down from her drug induced high so I knew I was about to get my butt beat something awful.

She said, "Bitch, you better watch your motherfucking tone when talking to me, you hear me?"

"I ain't no B," I responded courageously!

She walked a little closer to me with vigor and said, "You are what the fuck I say you are, you ugly ass bitch. Just like your black ass, sorry ass father!"

"My Daddy is cute and smart, and I am pretty like my Daddy. And my Daddy is not a drug addict like Mister Guy is." I nervously stated with teary eyes. My heart was pounding because I had a fear of her, but the hate I had for her drove me into a level of boldness that bordered the lines of disrespect through parental eyes.

I rolled my eyes. Rolled them hard while simultaneously rotating my neck. Next thing I felt was the slap of my mother's hand which sent me falling directly to the nasty, filthy carpet. While on the floor I was screaming and crying!

She said, "Oh okay bitch, I'mma give your ass something to cry for!"

She grabbed an extension cord from the bedroom and whipped me for a long time. I had cuts, lashes, and bruises all over my legs, arms, back, vagina area, head...everywhere! My stepfather was still in the room and eventually he came out. He screamed, "Wanda, stop beating on that girl like that," She paused for a moment to turn her verbal wrath on Guy, then proceeded to finish beating me. God, I wanted her to die!

■■■

It was the year of the attempted assassination on former President Ronald Reagan's life when Guy died of an overdose on the urine stained couch in my mother's terrible smelling apartment. Some months later, her new boo Petey, came on the scene. He was just as pitiful as Guy but sadder. Petey was constantly getting arrested and sent to jail. My mother was what some would call a *Ride or Die Chick.* That's a female who is committed and loyal to a man who is not worthy of the woman's faithfulness and devotion. I'm sitting here shaking my head at how silly she genuinely was for marrying those men who were ultimate failures.

Petey was sentenced to a couple of years in jail and was sent to serve his prison time at The Lorton Correctional Complex in Lorton, Virginia. There was a shuttle bus that picked up family and friends three days per week in Washington, DC. I was either ten or eleven years old, and I remember the bus would arrive in front of the *Woodward & Lothrop* building every Tuesday & Thursday evenings and Saturday mornings. My mother visited her boo faithfully, most times lugging my sister and I as if Petey was our papa. One particular weekday my mother didn't bring Tia. She wanted me to accompany her alone and she wanted to teach me how to "take work" inside of the facility. Unfortunately, Lorton Correctional was a very corrupt prison that DC natives affectionately called a "playground." It was closed in 2001.

She said, "LaWan, do not tell your black ass Daddy, you hear me? He's a punk, scared of every fucking thing, and I don't need no nigga trying to fuck up my hustle, you hear me?"

I just nodded my head submissively.

Before leaving the apartment, she rolled up what looked to be white powder in very super tiny sandwich bags. So small that no sandwich, even a sandwich cut in 24 pieces could fit inside. One aspirin could fit in the bag leaving no room for a second one, that's how small the plastic baggie was. I sat at the kitchen table with her as she taught me how to "cut work." Reiterating, not to tell my "Black ass Daddy" or my Aunt Denise, my grandmother or Uncle Tee; those were the adults who had loved me and had my best interest at heart. They were completely sane and would not side with this illegal, dysfunctional teaching that my own mother was instilling in me. After she cut up the heroin or it could've been cocaine, I'm not sure because she didn't specify, she placed the white, illegal substance in the baggies. She started telling me about my "job." She said, "LaWan, your job is to make sure your mother doesn't get caught, you understand? You and Tia are all I have." Surprisingly, she was speaking in the sweetest of tones; seemed sincere in that moment. I was convinced and deathly afraid at the same time. There was no disobeying mother! She wasn't the mother who asked, she was the mother who demanded and left the child with no choice.

My mother said, "Now, it's a good thing you have a big butt, cause it's gonna come in handy."

I had no idea what that meant. I was a child, so my childlike mind hadn't processed shapes and curves on females, especially not on me. She told me to stand up and pull down my jeans.

She said, "I'm going to place this work in between your butt cheeks, okay. You're a child, so the guards down Lorton ain't checking for you. I wrapped it good, but, don't start no fucking dramatics by scratching your ass and running your mouth talking 'bout your ass itching, you hear? Your father let you do all that drama shit with him, but don't try that shit with me, you hear?"

I shook my head vigorously up and down. She instructed me to lay down on the dirty couch face down. She opened my butt cheeks and placed the wrapped drugs in between them gently. I believe she placed five wrapped works there but I'm not positively sure.

"Stand up carefully LaWan. Clinch your butt cheeks and pull up your underwear and pants".

I did as I was told. Surprisingly the wrapped drugs didn't fall out. Grabbing what she needed, we headed out to meet the Lorton shuttle bus.

As usual the bus was crowded, with all African American women and children. Very few men were visiting prisoners, but I remember there were always a lot of women who obviously were very supportive. The passengers on the bus were loud and we didn't have a seat, so we had to hold on to the handrail for the entire ride, approximately 30-40 minutes. I remember having to pass gas, but I held it in. I remember having to urinate, but I held that too. I also held my peace by not sharing with my mother. When the bus pulled up at the prison's parking lot, we exited the bus. We walked inside the building and proceeded to line up behind those who was already there. Walking one by one through the metal detector my mother placed her purse on the table so the female guard could rummage through it. She also performed a pat down search on my mother. I noticed the security guard didn't search me as he didn't search other young children either. I never noticed that before since

It Ain't All Jokes!

I've been riding with my mother to see her loser boyfriends and husbands for a long time. Now that she's made me acutely aware of her mission and the dangers thereof, I was watching and unfortunately taking notes mentally. My brain was like a sponge, soaking up everything.

After going through the gate and walking down the hall through another huge metal door, we were escorted into the very large Visitors Hall. We sat on burnt orange colored chairs and waited for the guards to bring out prisoner Petey. He came out smiling as most of the prisoners who entered the visitor's hall did.

He spoke to me with a big smile, "Hey Lil' LaWan?" Rubbing my back like a proud stepdad, he asked, "Have you been a good girl in school?"

With a beautiful smile and a prepared lie, I answered, "Yes, I've been good." God knows my behavior had been terrible in school, but, I'm sure he didn't need to hear that. Plus, my mother probably would've knocked me to the ground if I said I'd been acting horribly in school.

Petey responded, "That's good babygirl. Always do good in school so you won't end up down here with your old man."

My mother didn't like what he said and interjected, "Damn Petey, the girl is going to the sixth grade, shit, you dropping all this deep shit on her as if she's going on twenty-one years old."

He took a deep frustrated breath and said, "Alright Wanda, damn!"

They began to talk casually as I looked around wanting to play with the other kids. My mother knew a lot of the prisoners by name as most yelled over to her saying, "What's up Fat Wanda?"

"What's up Wanda girl, why you ain't bring that big butt Loretta down here with you, man, you know I'm trying to be her man," A prisoner yelled excitedly.

"Hey Wanda, did you get that message to tall Steve," another concerned prisoner asked.

All kinds of playful and serious questions were thrown at my mother. She smirked and responded to every prisoner accordingly. I viewed her as the *go-to* woman for prisoners who needed connections to the outside world. She was very ready to assist in any way possible. They were prisoners who felt more like family to her and it showed. A prisoner's visiting hall that allowed hands on visits is no place for a small child. It was not a place that I should've been exposed to, especially given the fact that my Daddy wasn't a prisoner. He was home, obeying laws and striving to live his best life. There were too many adult, Rated-R conversations and language that no child should've been subjected to hear, absorb, nor remember.

My mother gave me a strange look. It was a look whereas I had to read her body language. Mind you, I'm eleven years old, so I had to grow up quickly. Instead of being home playing on the playground, doing homework, or watching cartoons, I was forced to be a drug dealer's assistant.

She spoke almost robotic when she asked, "LaWan, do you need to use the bathroom?"

Before I could answer, she said "Yeah you do, let's go."

She grabbed my hand in a loving way and we walked through a door that lead to the ladies room. There were two or three stalls which all were unoccupied. My mother and I went into the last stall that was further from the door.

She whispered, "Pull your pants down and bend over slightly."

I did as I was told. She removed the drugs from in between my sweaty, stinky, butt cheeks. After I pulled up my pants, she flushed the toilet.

Then she whispered, "Just in case somebody is listening, flushing the toilet will throw them off."

I had no idea what she was talking about, I just listened and remembered as she would often say, "I'm teaching you something and I'm only going to show you one time."

My fear was that I wouldn't learn the first time and as a result I would get a beating. In my young mind, I just didn't want a beating. Pain was not my friend. That woman hits hard and she displayed no mercy, so my brain had to comprehend well.

My mother put the wrapped drugs into her mouth, more specifically underneath of her tongue. Yuck!

She said, "Come on! When we go back out here don't say a word to nobody about what went on in here, you hear me?"

I responded, "Yes."

We walked back into the Visitor's Hall and it seemed that a lot of people were beginning to leave. She went over to Petey and they started to hug one another affectionately and whisper in each other's ears. An announcement was made over the speaker, letting everybody know visiting hours were coming to an end. We proceeded to walk slowly towards the exit. Many women started to kiss their men goodbye. Long, tongue kisses. I would stand and watch intensely. My mother and Petey started kissing. They kissed for a few minutes as I watched.

It Ain't All Jokes!

Other kids watched, babies cried, kids pulled on their mother's legs, and some kids were still running around in small circles near their moms having the time of their lives. I remember wondering where were the dirty, butt smelling drugs? Curiosity began to get the better of me as I was now about to ask my mother. She must've detected my next move, because she turned to me, bent her back until we were eye-to-eye, and said through clinched teeth and a harsh low whisper,

"LaWan!! Don't ask me shit right now because you know what I said to you. Don't get yourself fucked up in here, do you understand me?"

I nodded my head in fear of my understanding. Later I learned when she tongued kissed Petey, that was her way of passing the drugs from her mouth to his. He would swallow them and later regurgitate them after returning to his cell without the prying eyes of the guards. The amazing power of addiction! Addictions will have a person selling their mind, body and soul to the Devil...literally.

■■■

My mother instructed me to pick up my little sister after school each day. When class dismissed, I would walk to my sister's classroom to retrieve her and then we would head home together. I had my own door key. The keys hung on a chain around my neck. I was responsible in the fact that I never lost my keys. Still to this day, I've never lost a key neither have I misplaced one either. The fear of Wanda yet haunts me, I guess.

When we arrived home, there was a handwritten note with the neatest and prettiest penmanship on the table that read: *"Dear LaWan! Do not open the door for anyone. I will call you. Remember the code? I'm not repeating it again. Feed Tia and feed yourself. I'll see ya'll tonight. Love ya, Wanda."*

Let me explain to you what the *code* was. Whenever she wasn't home I was instructed never to answer the phone. Tia was too young to answer the phone in my mother's opinion. My mother would call and let the phone ring two times. She would then hang up. After ten seconds the phone would ring again then I knew that was her and I would answer. Whew...this woman made life hard for a young daughter. Geesh!!

It Ain't All Jokes!

So, I read the note out loud to Tia and asked, "What do you want to eat," as she followed me into the small filthy kitchen.

Roaches were everywhere and the sun was still shining inside of the cramped apartment. I opened the refrigerator and saw old leftovers in a bowl; however, it had a smell that spoke to my young senses warning me not to eat its contents. Our stomachs were growling badly but there was no food. My mother didn't come home that night neither did she call. The next day we woke up for school. All our clothes were dirty. As a matter of fact, my underwear was so soiled that my vagina had developed a rash which caused me to scratch uncontrollably. I changed my extremely mucky panties and put on a pair that wasn't as dirty, retrieving them from the dirty clothes hamper. More like the floor since the clothes in the hamper spilled over onto the floor inside of the even dirtier closet. I gave my sister a pair of lesser dirty underwear to change into as well. We dressed in unclean clothes and went to school.

Three days later, my mother still hadn't returned home, and Friday had arrived. Fridays are the days I looked forward to going over my Daddy's house for the weekend! I always got super excited being that my Daddy's house held love, peace, happiness, food, fun, good sleep…and I got a chance to take a warm bubble bath! Since I hadn't received instructions from my mother about what to do with my sister, I picked her up from her classroom and headed home.

I called my Daddy at home. When he answered I said, "Daddy, my mother hasn't come home all week. I don't know what to do with Tia. Should I call Aunt Denise?"

Aunt Denise is my mother's oldest sister and she was always a very positive help and influence in our lives. For as long as I could remember, I wished Aunt Denise had been our mom. We loved her dearly and she was our favorite aunt. I was such a mature young girl. *Growing up Wanda* will bring out the survivor in you!

Daddy answered, "No, just hop on the bus sweetheart and bring your sister with you."

"Okay, Daddy," I responded.

My sister and I caught the number 42 bus marked Stadium Armory. We got off at 18th Street & Columbia Road, N.W. After exiting the bus, we boarded our final bus marked number 94 Stanton Road. I'm unsure how long the ride was, but we arrived at my Dad's humble, super clean, Pine-Sol aroma smelling apartment safely. Daddy was super excited to see me, gave me and hug and kiss on the forehead. And he showed my sister equal the love he showed me.

Monday came too quickly and back to school my sister and I returned. We had on clean underwear and clothes, and our hair was combed neatly. I hated going to my mother's house, so I started crying and complaining that I didn't want to go to school, adding that my stomach hurt. Daddy knew I didn't have a tummy ache. He promised that he's working on gaining custody and encouraged me to hold on a little while longer.

"LaWan, you have to love your mother and pray for her, okay", is what he said.

"NO, I HATE HER," is what I yelled! I meant every word too.

After school I picked up my sister from her classroom and we walked to my mother's apartment. I remembered my Dad told me if my mother wasn't home to call him and he would bring us food to eat. She wasn't there so I rushed to the telephone that was mounted on the kitchen wall and dialed Dad.

"Yo, Mike speaking," Dad answered in his signature greeting.

"Daddy, she's not here. Tia and I are hungry. Can you bring us McDonald's," I rattled off as fast as I could.

"Sure, daughter, stay put and I'll see you both shortly," he promised.

I hung up knowing my Daddy was on his way. He always kept his promises and I could depend on him for anything. He never let me down! Daddy showed up with our McDonald's. My sister had a happy meal with an orange soda. I had a Big Mac, small fries and a strawberry shake. Daddy knew what I loved, and he knew what would make me happy. He looked around the filthy kitchen, living room and dining room area. He didn't say anything negative, but I could only imagine what was going through his mind. On the table there was an ashtray full of cigarette butts, dirty cups, empty beer cans, candy wrappers, unpaid bills, unopened mail, notes from our teachers, roaches crawling, and dead roaches needing to be buried. The table was made of glass that hadn't seen glass cleaner since its days in the furniture store. The four chairs that matched the table had steel legs that were still intact.

Daddy cleared two spots on the table so that my sister and I could eat our dinner. He sat with us and basically watched me with a slight smile with love in his eyes. Tia and I happily talked non-stop. He listened attentively and responded when needed. Daddy was engaging and treated my sister as if she was his daughter too. My mother was truly blessed to have created a child with such an amazing man like my Daddy!

The phone rang two full times then stopped. At least a minute later it rang again, and I was a little apprehensive to answer because it wasn't the *code*. My mother always called back no more than ten seconds after two full rings. But I took a chance and answered anyway.

"You have a collect call from Wanda, will you accept," the operator asked.

"LaWan, it's me, accept the charges," my mother's voiced boomed.

"Okay, I accept the charges," I responded.

"Go ahead caller," the operator responded, then hung up.

I was so excited about having my Daddy a few feet away and the delicious McDonald's food, that I forgot about my mother's crazy rules.

"Mommy, my Daddy is here, and he bought me and Tia McDonald's food because you were gone and we were hungry," I innocently said as only a child would.

"What the fuck?! You got that nigga Mike in my motherfuckin' house? Are you fuckin' crazy," she yelled into the receiver?

I was frightened to death and I felt torn as I thought my Daddy was afraid of her just like I was and we together would get beaten down.

"LaWan, by the time I get home that mothertucker betta not be in my house! Did he go through my shit? Did he go in my fucking room? See, this is the shit I'm talking about. This nigga is gonna use this shit in court. The fuck! Look, tell his black ass he gotta go now, LaWan!"

"Yes, mommy," I responded meekly.

Then she slammed the phone in my ear. I turned to my Daddy and started crying. Either he heard her screams through the phone, or he knew it was time that he left.

"Daddy, I don't want you to go. Please take me with you," I begged with real tears in my eyes!

Daddy held me close and said, "LaWan, stay strong for yourself and for Tia. Stop crying baby girl. Soon and very soon you'll be able to live with me. Hang in there real tough, okay," His voice was gentle, soothing and made me feel safe.

"Okay." I assured Dad. Still crying uncontrollably.

I later learned that my mother had flew to Jamaica with a random dude she met in a Reggae club. She had been gone for over a week. How could she just take off and leave without making sure her children were taken care of? Clearly, that woman didn't want us. Where was

It Ain't All Jokes!

Child Protective Service when we needed them? That woman pretended to be a mother who wanted her children, but her actions showed otherwise.

■■■

The holiday season was approaching as Christmas was drawing near. I had already given my Daddy a lengthy Christmas list, written neatly and numbered from one to fifty. Yep, there were fifty things I desired, and my Daddy never disappointed me. Did I mention I was extremely spoiled? Yep, my Daddy spoiled me but not my mother. I was looking forward to spending the Christmas break with my Daddy in peace with love in the air, clean linen on the bed, food on the table, and bubbles in the bathtub. My vision was so clear that anxiety would always overwhelm me at the happy thoughts of going to Daddy's house.

This particular year my sister asked if she could go with me to my Daddy's house. Immediately I said, "no." I just didn't want to share my Daddy! I'm unsure how it all came together but my sister ended up going to my Daddy's house with me for the winter break. Christmas was amazing and I received every gift on my long, outrageous list. My sister had a few gifts as well from my Dad and Aunt Denise. School was closed for two weeks.

When the first Monday of January came, it was time for us to return to school. Daddy called my mother, but he didn't get an answer.

He said, "LaWan, I'm not sure where Wanda is, but, after school I want you and Tia to catch the bus back to my house, okay?"

"Okay, Daddy," I responded with a smile. After school I picked up my sister from her classroom and headed to the bus stop, bypassing the apartment building where my mother resided. This ritual went on for roughly two months! No one heard from my mother at all.

The telephone rings and my Dad answers. I watched my Daddy sigh, take in a deep breath and say, "Sure, I'll accept the charges." My mother had called collect. She had been locked up since the Christmas break began. Probably for a drug possession, maybe fighting or something violent. At any rate, she told Daddy that she was on her way to pick up Tia. She never came.

A few days later, Daddy asked me, "LaWan, where does your mother typically hang out? She was supposed to pick Tia up days ago."

"She hangs out on 14th & V Street, Daddy. That's where she sells drugs. If she's not there, you can find her at Miss Peggy's house. She's the dope lady with the dope house on W Street. My mother sometimes would send me to Peggy's house to get her works," I told Daddy not leaving out any details.

I was snitching! I hated her! She demonstrated to me absolutely no love, so my loyalty was to my Daddy only. He had a stunned and almost heartbreaking look on his face as he learned of the adult knowledge that I knew about the life of a drug addict. I was a young child and should not have been privy to any of this stuff.

Daddy, my sister, and I climbed into Dad's 1974 brown Chrysler Imperial. The car was huge. The seats were leather and long like my grandmother's couch. At least fourteen small children could sit across the back comfortably. My sister and I sat up front while daddy drove. We reached our destination at 14th & V Streets, NW, and Daddy parked. There was a huge crowd of drug addicts and drug dealers gathered outside and inside of a store. The drug dealers who were addicts were softly promoting the name of the drug in which they were selling.

"Rohi, Rohi, Rohi," is one name a junkie called out.

"I got that Blaze. Shit real good," an addict said with a slur, who was visibly high as he was nodding and practically sleep standing up, due to the effects of heroin.

My Daddy never sold or used drugs. This atmosphere was not one that he found comfortable.

Somehow, he remained brave enough to tread through it in search of my mother.

"Daddy, there's my mother right there," I shouted happily, pointing my finger when I spotted my mother.

She was strolling inside of the store and we followed her inside. When we walked in, we saw another woman who huddled up behind my mother as if using her body as a shield. My mother reached down inside her sweatpants and underwear, retrieving drugs from in between her butt cheeks. That was her famous hiding place. The woman and my mother discreetly exchanged the drugs and the money with the same hand, then the woman turned to leave. When my mother looked around, she spotted us. My sister ran to my mother in an attempt to give her a hug but stopped short because of the foul look on my mother's face. Hugging and showing affection was a no-no with my mother. I stood beside my Daddy unfazed. I would never attempt to hug her. Not ever!

"Wanda, where have you been? You said you were coming to pick up Tia and you never did," my Daddy asked in his deep baritone voice.

"Fuck you doing bringing my kids up here, Mike? I don't play that shit!"

With an incredulous look, Daddy responded, "Wanda, you've got to be kidding me. How in the world

It Ain't All Jokes!

would I know about this god forsaken place if you hadn't introduced this life to LaWan? Look, let me grab Tia's bag from the car and get home."

I followed Daddy through the haze of cigarette smoke and out of the unsanitary store door. My mother followed us with my sister in tow.

Starting trouble my mother said with venom, "Bitch ass nigga acting like you better than me! You ain't better than me, Mike. Trying to turn my motherfucking daughter against me. Nigga, I should get my crew to bash your motherfuckin' skull in!"

"Look Wanda, here are Tia's bags," he said, and he handed her Tia's bags.

"LaWan, get in the car so we can go," he said to me.

In that moment I thought my Daddy was a punk. I wanted him to fight my mother and any of those goons she was threatening to use to attack him. He opened the car door for me as I smiled and waved goodbye to Tia. I looked at my mother and rolled my eyes. Yes indeed, I was showing off big time!

"Oh bitch, don't show off because you're with your black ass Daddy! I'll still fuck you up," my mother said to me. Daddy's car couldn't start up fast enough. That woman was demented, and I was scared!

Petey was released from jail again. My mother didn't seem impressed. They argued non-stop and when he would be quiet, she kept yelling, cussing, and threatening him. Such a loser! The both of them together!

Petey and my mother were in the bedroom with the door closed. Shooting dope per usual. I was in the living room watching a hilarious episode of *Good Times* on the 13-inch black & white television. My mother came barreling out of the bedroom in a panic. She was sweating and moving around frantically. My heart skipped a beat as I thought she was going to grab a belt and begin beating me. But she didn't, thank God!

"Wan? Look! Petey ass done fucked up and OD'd! Help me get his body up outta here! Shit, his ass can't die in here!" She spoke fast and fearful. This was the first time I've ever seen her scared and I felt a different kind of fear. The kind of fear that left me wondering who was in control. But, in true Wanda fashion, she was quick-witted and could think fast on her feet. She started strategizing a plan in her mind. That DNA gene was passed on to me. She instructed me to follow her into the unkept bedroom. Petey was spawled out on the floor with a syringe needle hanging from his neck. I can't remember if she pulled it out or left it there because I was distracted by his penis hanging out of his pants, so my young, innocent, virgin eyes were staring widely.

"Grab his arms and pull him," she demanded!

I tried, but I was 11 years old with the strength of a seven-year-old girl, so how was I going to pull a grown man?

She snapped in frustration, "Move LaWan! Go into the living room!"

I rushed into the living scared for my own life. With the strength of a determined Wonder Woman, she started dragging Petey by both arms. The syringe was no longer in his neck and his penis was tucked back into his dingy jeans. She was sweating and her mouth appeared to be dry. She looked out of the apartment door peep hole. Then she opened the door and stepped into the hallway looking around. Our building was a fairly quiet one with the exception of the constant commotion coming from our dysfunctional unit.

She stepped back into the apartment and explained, "Wan, we've got to get Petey out of here. Let's take him to the alley, okay? So, I want you to hold this door open."

I did as I was told.

Our apartment was on the second floor. Two flights of steps up from the basement. My mother started dragging him down the stairs. Carefully protecting his head. That woman was super strong! Petey was a petite man, probably weighing all of 140 pounds soak and wet. We got to the basement and in front of the laundry room door.

"Wan? Look inside to see if somebody's in there." She spoke in a conspirator whisper.

I opened the laundry room door and as luck would have it....it was empty! Mercy was on my mother's side. I held the door open while my mother dragged Petey's seemingly lifeless body into the laundry room then out of the basement door which lead to the alley. She left him in the alley. We both walked up to the apartment and she started cleaning up. I believe it was nervous energy because she never cleaned up before. We had no Pine-Sol, bleach, dishwashing liquid, a broom, mop, vacuum cleaner, Windex or soap. But she started rearranging stuff and throwing things in the trash can. She grabbed her RC soda from the refrigerator and lit a Kool cigarette to calm her nerves.

The soda and the cigarette were doing a fantastic job on easing her anxiety. She called me over to her and spoke precisely and directly.

It Ain't All Jokes!

"LaWan! Do not tell your father or anybody else about what happened to Petey. Bottom line, the nigga can't handle the good shit and it took him out. So, what goes on in this house stays in this house. Do you understand me?"

"Yes, mommy," I responded.

Sitting back on the sofa wondering if Petey was still in the alley, I couldn't focus on the next television program, *What's Happening*. I remember my mind was racing. *Bang, bang, bang* someone pounded on the door! The pounding caused my mother and I to both jump nervously. My mother tiptoed to the door, peeked through the peep hole, tiptoed over to me and whispered in my ear and with cigarette smelling breath she said, "That's the police. Do not say one damn word."

As she walked back towards the door, she spoke loudly in a proper tone, "Who is it?"

"It's the Metropolitan Police Department ma'am. Can you open the door?"

My mother looked at me and put her finger over her lips, indicating to me to keep my lips zipped.

She opened the door. Standing on the other side was two African American police officers and Petey! Yep Petey! Out from the grave he arose! I was scared to death when I saw Petey and almost screamed. I was a nervous wreck.

"Ma'am, we found this gentleman in the alley unconscious. We revived him and insisted that he goes to the hospital, but he insisted he was okay and wanted to go home. He said he lives here, that his wife is Wanda and that his wife and stepdaughter dragged him to the alley to die." The first officer responded.

"That's fucked up what yall did to me Wanda," Petey spoke.

"Oh my God, Petey, you're getting high again," my mother said with proper diction and a leveled head.

She turned to the police officers and said, "Officers, thank you very much for finding my husband. We had no clue where he was, and I didn't worry because the hour is still young." Give this woman an Oscar.

"Ma'am, may we come inside? I'd like to meet his stepdaughter, please." Officer number two asked.

"Sure." My mother stepped aside, and all three men came in.

Petey turned to me, "LaWan, that's fucked up you helped your mother do that shit to me, young blood. You know I treat you and Tia good and you did me dirty as shit, LaWan."

My mother had fire in her eyes but remained silent. I didn't say anything. Officer number two asked me, "How old are you young lady?"

It Ain't All Jokes!

"Eleven," I answered politely. Hoping I wouldn't get in trouble with my mother. Afterall, she told me to keep my mouth closed.

"Okay, well, that will be all. Sir, get some help. Ma'am, thank you for your cooperation and you all have a good day," Officer number two spoke to all of us. My mother thanked both officers and they left. She walked to the large window and peeked out until the officers were in their squad car. When they pulled off, she turned around and punched Petey directly in the jaw and didn't stop attacking him until he hit the floor. I was stunned and just sat still. After she got winded, she stood over Petey and said, "Nigga, don't ever OD in here again! And yeah, me and my motherfucking daughter dragged your dumb ass outside. Hot ass bringing cops to my house. I see why your dirty ass always locked up!" She was pissed off mad and Petey was bleeding and looking for a tooth that she knocked out. I was quietly sitting on the couch feeling the need to urinate but holding it.

■■■

My mother had been evicted from the dirty apartment on Mount Pleasant Street and moved into the house of Ms. Carol on Euclid Street, NW. It was a 3-story yellow brick rowhouse that Ms. Carol kept clean and neat. We occupied two of the bedrooms on the third floor of the house. Ms. Carol had one child, a son named Craig, who was super cool and fun to play with in the house. We were the same age. Unfortunately, Craig had been shot and killed in a drug related drive-by in Washington, DC a few years later.

One Sunday evening Daddy dropped me back home after spending a fabulous weekend with him. I started crying as we ascended the stairs towards the huge black door.

"Daddy, I hate her, and I want to live with you!"

"LaWan, please stop crying daughter," Daddy urged gently. He continued in an assuring tone, "The court case is coming up and I believe the judge will rule in our favor by granting me full custody of you. But continue to be a good girl, try to stay out of your mother's way, and take notes of anything that makes you uncomfortable so we can discuss it, okay?"

"Okay Daddy," I sniff as tears continued to fall from my eyes.

He knocked on the door. When my mother answered I screamed and cried as loud as I could! I grabbed Daddy's waist in an effort of getting my way so he would somehow change his mind and allow me my heart's desire, to return home with him. He began to pry my arms from around his waist talking in soft, loving tones in hopes of soothing my damaged soul. My mother just looked. Not saying a mumbling word. Her arms were folded as if the dramatics of it all was making her sick to her stomach. She was an evil woman who showed no compassion and could careless either way.

Daddy kissed me goodbye and I reluctantly walked inside.

"Get your spoiled ass upstairs now, bitch! Making all that fucking noise like that nigga is father of the fucking year. I'mma show yo ass your father ain't shit and don't run shit," my mother said to me with as much venom as a rattlesnake.

I went into the bedroom and sat down quietly. Hoping beyond hope that she would not beat me. I knew she would because when she spoke threats to beat, punch, smack, or hit me, she fulfilled every one of them. Even if it meant waking up in the middle of the night to whoop me, she was would maintain her word.

She came into the bedroom with a white extension cord in her hand.

"Didn't I tell you to stop all that fuckin' crying when your black ass Daddy brings you home? Huh? Didn't I? Yelling and fuckin' screaming like you are better than me. Bitch, your father got your head swole thinkin' you are the only motherfucker around here that's cute and shit! Well, I'm about to show you who's the fuckin' boss and it ain't yo Daddy! Take your fuckin' clothes off!"

I stood up slowly while crying.

"Mommy, I promise I won't cry no mo' when my Daddy brings me home," I pleaded as I cried.

"LaWan, I'm not gonna tell you again, take your motherfuckin' clothes off now!"

I pulled down my jeans slowly. She snatched my jeans from my ankles causing my socks and shoes to become entangled as she tossed all the garments to the side. *"Swoosh, swoosh, swoosh...",* were the brutal sounds vibrating the air as the lashes landed on my tender skin. My mother was swinging that extension cord as if I was the Messiah on the cross dying for the remission of sin. My mother swung hard. Swinging like a mad woman with the power to take her daughter's life away. I was screaming, crying, jumping around, falling on the floor then jumping back up on my feet, begging her to stop, and begging anyone who could hear me to help me! Ms. Carol came running up to the third floor.

"Wanda? What the hell? You're going to kill that girl! Stop beating LaWan like that!" Ms. Carol said in an authoritative tone.

It Ain't All Jokes!

Stopping mid swing, "Look Carol, mind yo fuckin' business! LaWan is my daughter. You betta worry about Craig's ass. This ass right here came outta my pussy!" My mother spewed.

"I don't care who pussy LaWan came out of, you cannot beat on that girl like that in here, Wanda. Fuck that! You're going to have to move doing shit like that. No wonder Mike trying to take her ass from you!" Carol responded even bolder.

They began to argue back and forth, which was a total relief for me because my mother didn't resume beating me. I laid down in the twin bed across from my sister and pretended to be sleep. After the argument ended, Carol went back downstairs as my mother walked into her bedroom slamming the door.

The next day I left out for school. My legs were burning badly and were hot. Felt like fire underneath of my blue jeans. After school I didn't have to pick my sister up, so I went to my play Aunt's house on Quincy Street. It was a hot Monday in June and she instructed me to go into the bathroom and change into a pair of shorts. She handed me the shorts and I went into the bathroom. I pulled down my too tight jeans that were obviously too small. To my shock and utter surprise, my skin peeled off my legs as I pulled my jeans down. I cried when I saw the blood and nearly white meat where the gashes were visible from the force of the extension cord beating. One of my play cousins turned the unlocked door of the bathroom and came inside without knocking. When she saw my legs, she immediately ran downstairs to tell our aunt. My aunt questioned me then called my Daddy immediately and the police.

Later that day I was taken to the police station and both Daddy and I were questioned by a detective. Pictures of my legs were taken. Immediately my mother was ordered never to hit me again. Other than giving me a hug, she could not put her hands on me. It was such a relief to hear that life changing news!

Wanda never let up on the verbal assault though. I was still called a whore, bitch, stupid, dumb, nappy headed, ugly feet, and big mouth. I was also told I will probably end up like her "junkie ass" if I don't watch my steps. Whatever that was supposed to mean.

I was a bully growing up. Which was partly encouraged by my mother. She was a bully and I mimicked a lot of whatever she would do and say to people, especially to me and my sister. I was always fighting growing up. It seemed I could never keep friends, especially females. I could make them but keeping them was a challenge. I was always the one to cause ruckus in the friendship causing it to end. Either I would say something hateful or do something evil to them. The few female friends I had in elementary school and most of junior high school were the ones who was afraid to end the friendship because they understood it would result in a fistfight that I would start. Or, they just felt sorry for me. I just didn't know how to be a friend to females. I had no example! It's interesting that I would often gravitate to males. Males are still my favorite! I LOVE MEN! My Daddy was such a positive and wholesome example of how a woman is supposed to be treated by a man, that I naturally loved males and always wanted to be in their presence. Now, let's be clear, I had my share of arguments and fistfights with boys too, but the fights were rare and far between. Talking, laughing, and being around boys made me smile and bought happiness to my heart.

IF GOD NEVER SAVED ME...
MY DADDY WAS MORE THAN ENOUGH!

"LaWan, we are going down to see a psychiatrist. She's going to talk with you about me, your mother and your school. Be very honest with her, okay dear heart," Daddy said to me one weekday morning.

"Okay, Daddy," I responded happily.

I wore a pretty dress, tights, and patent leather shoes that were new. They fit perfectly. My feet were wide and every so often shoes didn't fit properly. Daddy would purchase my shoes from *Boyce & Lewis*. A specialty store that sold hard bottomed walkers for toddlers as well as shoes that catered to wide width feet of all ages. The few pair of shoes that my mother purchased were never from any specialty stores. The shoes were always too tight plus, they caused my toes to develop corns at a young age. She didn't care and I was not allowed to share my issues with her.

It Ain't All Jokes!

If shoes didn't fit correctly and I voiced that concern, my mother would say, "Well, your ass either take these or you don't get nothing! Your ugly ass feet will stretch them out. Girl, you gotta break shoes in."

Feeling desperate with no options, I accepted the too tight shoes in hopes that my wide feet would stretch them out. Most times they did.

Daddy and I took the number 70 bus going south from 7th & Florida Avenue, NW, and exited the bus at 7th & G Streets, NW. We walked into a tall white building, entered the elevator and got off on our intended floor. After signing in at the reception desk, we sat down in the small waiting area a few steps away.

"Mr. Taylor," a pretty white woman with long sandy blond hair called out from an opened door.

Daddy grabbed my hand and we walked toward the woman.

"Hi, I'm Michael Taylor and this is my daughter LaWan Taylor," Daddy spoke in a professional tone as he extended his hand to shake her hand.

With a professional smile, she informed us that she would be our mediation case manager for the custody hearing.

We followed her into a very nice office that smelled like flowers and perfume from Avon. My grandmother wore the same fragrance, so I was familiar with the scent. Fresh smells became an obsession of mine, due to my mother's always unpleasant smelling apartment and body odor.

"You must be LaWan," the psychiatrist stated with the most pleasant and assuring smile. I nodded shyly.
"Don't nod your head baby girl," my Daddy urged gently.
"Yes," I answered.
She explained who she was and the purpose of the meeting. Then she asked my Daddy to exit the room and that the interview shouldn't take no more than an hour. The psychiatrist offered me a soft drink which I happily accepted. She proceeded to ask me questions about my school, my siblings, my friends, and my parents. Spending a great deal of questions on my parents, especially my mother. Some of the questions I can't remember but some I do.

"So, do you like having your own bedroom at your mom's house," She asked.
"I don't have my own room. Me and my sister sleep on the rollaway bed," I corrected.

It Ain't All Jokes!

Perplexed, the woman looked down at her notes on the yellow legal pad, then asked, "the rollaway bed? What do you mean?"

"I sleep at the top and my sister sleep at the bottom. My mother and Petey sleep in the bed," I explained.

By this time my mother had moved out of Ms. Carol's nice house into a shabby rooming house. I remember the woman writing lots of notes as I spoke. It's obvious my mother had lied to her about our living arrangements.

A month or two before 5th grade ended, my Daddy was awarded with the exciting news that he had won full custody of me and I was to move directly in with him on the last day of school, effective June of that year. When he shared the news with me, I was sooo ecstatic! I smiled and danced around like a lottery winner! I didn't know God as my personal savior, but after attending church Sunday after Sunday with my grandmother, I knew enough to know God had answered our prayer!

After school I picked up my sister and shared.

"Tia, I'm leaving y'all. My Daddy got custody of me and I'm moving with my Daddy on the last day of school. You probably won't ever see me again," I said cheerfully smiling hard.

"LaWan, please don't leave. I want you to stay with me," my sister responded sadly.

"Nope! Ma abuses us and beats us and I hate her, so I'm leaving," I said with determination.

I packed up my small amount of unclean clothes, stuffed them in plastic Safeway bags and placed them near the front door. I knew I would be leaving before long, so I had already checked out in my mind. My mother came home, and I started to rattle off my thrilling news to her as if she hadn't received the official court documents.

"First of all...", she grabs the three bags of clothes and slung them away from the door. "...Put that shit somewhere because that trash ain't sitting by my fuckin' door," she yelled.

I remember not feeling bad or hurt. I remember my heart feeling very hard and numb towards her. I didn't care anymore. I was leaving there for good in hopes of never laying eyes on her again!

■■

"LaWan, what do you want for dinner," my Daddy asked me.

"Ice cream and cake," I answered happily.

It Ain't All Jokes!

Ice cream and cake is what I had too. My daddy spoiled me to the point that he gave me any and everything I wanted. I never ate a balanced diet because I loved fried food and junk foods. My daily diet consisted of cold cereal, (preferably Foot Loops), Popeyes chicken, McDonalds, cake, ice cream, cookies, and peanut butter & jelly sandwiches. I hated vegetables, except corn on the cob, and disliked baked food, so he never forced me to eat any.

Living with Daddy was a dream come true. Daddy lived in a super clean two-bedroom apartment. He gave me the largest room. I had two twin beds in my room. A Dallas Cowboys flannel sheet set on one bed and some other blue blankets on the other. My room was painted sky blue and it was pretty. I had lots of clothes, shoes, toys, my own colored television and my very own Snoopy telephone. It was the life I had always dreamed about! It was the life I deserved. Every child deserves to be adored and treated with love. Afterall, children didn't ask to be born, they are a gift sent from God.

Soon after gaining total custody of me, Daddy landed a job working for Metro (Washington Metropolitan Area Transit Authority). He said the salary was more than public school teacher's and he needed more money as a full-time custodial parent. While working as a teacher, he also worked part-time for a salon cleaning up nightly. I remember going with him to work some evenings which was fun. Being with my Daddy all the time was all that I've ever wanted. To feel loved and treated like royalty. Is that too much for a child to desire?

The custody agreement was that I would spend weekends with my mother, one month in the summer, and rotate Thanksgiving and Christmas holidays. I didn't want to spend none of those days with her. EVER! Most weekends I would spend at my grandmother's house. Grandmother Pauline loved the Lord! Her life and lifestyle mirrored that of Jesus Christ. She was a woman who walked by faith and not by sight. Totally dependent on God for everything. I viewed her as a strict grandmother that rarely smiled, never joked, and was always serious about matters in life. She didn't have any gray areas. Either a situation was God ordained or a situation was the Devil sent. My grandmother taught me stories in the Bible, how to pray, and I had to study scriptures and recite them verbatim. She took me to church every Sunday. Often, she would quote, *As for me and my house, we will serve the Lord,* so being absent from church was not an option. I hated going to church! It was unexciting to me. The only enjoyable things about church that I discovered was dinner in the fellowship hall after benediction! My grandmother had a best friend, Mrs. Betty Taylor, who became my Godmother. Mrs. Betty Taylor loved me to life! In my heart I wanted her to be my mother! I was a perfect fit into her family, and it was ironic that we shared the same last name.

Daddy rarely attended church, but he made sure I attended every Sunday. And I mean E V E R Y SUNDAY! Lol There was no escaping church and I was annoyed about going. Dad would attend every Easter Sunday and he'd attend if I was in a program at church. He was always supportive. There was never a time that I could remember not having my Daddy in attendance! If no one else in the audience was there to support me, Daddy was visibly present!

Daddy took me on lots of trips. If he didn't take me himself, he would pay for the excursion so I could attend. I remember going to Montego Bay, Jamaica for the first time at age 11. I remember it being fun with my favorite cousin Teedar and the weather being extremely hot! Kings Dominion, Busch Gardens, and Hershey Park were my favorite places to go every spring and summer. I loved Atlantic City too. I was an expert swimmer at a very young age, so I loved to swim!

Daddy kept me active. I was on the cheerleading team for years, in gymnastics class for four years, a majorette for a year, ballet class for less than four months, took two years of tennis lessons, and on the swim team for years. I loved playing all sports and although snowball fighting wasn't a sport, I was good at that too! My aggressive behavior caused me to get kicked out of ballet class. To my defense, I didn't like ballet anyway. Daddy supported my dreams no matter how ridiculous they sounded. As long I could remember, I wanted to be a Dallas Cowboys Cheerleader. Daddy said, "Daughter, you can be whatever you want to be." He failed to tell me that DNA would cause my hips to spread and the likelihood of me fitting into a size 4 uniform was pretty much never going to happen, but, Daddy was a supporter. I also wanted to be a police officer. I said to Daddy, "I want to be a cop so I can lock my mother up." Again, Dad's response was, "Daughter, you can be whatever you want to be." Dad's such the optimist.

  Daddy worked the night shift, 11:00pm-7:00am. I was left home by myself five days a week. It wasn't a wise decision on his part, but I presume he was left with no choice. I did have two cats, Tracey & Stacey, that kept me company. Daddy had asked our neighbor Ms. Carolyn to listen in on me during the night. Sadly, her ex-boyfriend Mr. Charles used to beat on her. I would hear her scream for her life. She often would have black eyes, missing teeth, swollen jaw and even a broken arm or two. Ms. Carolyn ended up losing her mind and became homeless living on the street. If she's still alive, I pray she is well.

It Ain't All Jokes!

Thanks be to God that fires never broke out in our home and burglars never broke in. I knew I had a praying grandmother and godmother! But what I did let in the house was boys. Oh yeah! I loved boys and by this time I'm entering my teen years, so puberty had me looking at boys differently from the way I looked at them in elementary school. Lust had filled my eyes and boys looked delicious to me!

I lost my virginity at age 14. And I lost it on my twin bed with the Dallas Cowboys flannel cover and sheets. I'm not going to say his name because I lied to the second guy, telling him he was my first. And if he's reading this, I don't want his feelings hurt, or his ego bruised. Oh well. It's what most of us young girls did…we lied about our number of sex partners!

CHRONICLES OF WANDA...

"Hello," I answered the phone.

"LaWan, what are you doing," my mother asked.

"Nothing, watching TV."

"Look, tomorrow I'mma need you to skip school and go with me down to the court building. I've gotta take a urine and I need to use your pee so I won't get stepped back, okay?"

With a deep sigh, I responded, "Okay." Then I added, "I want some new Guess jeans. The pair I want are in *Up Against The Wall* and my Daddy said I've gotta put them in layaway and that's stupid, so can you buy them?"

"Damn! Alright," my mother said with a grunt as if she really didn't want to agree with my terms.

At this point in our farce of a mother-daughter relationship I started asking her for money or material things if she wanted me to do something illegal for her. It was an unspoken understanding that we had developed with one another. Whether picking up drugs from her dealer friends or transporting drugs from city to city. And now she's added urine donation to my lengthy, growing illegal resumé.

The next day I pretended to get ready for school, only to leave out of the house to meet my mother at the United States Municipal Courthouse. We walked to the corner of 5th & Indiana Avenue, NW and she started explaining.

"When we go inside, follow me to the courtroom, but don't talk to me or sit beside me. When you see me get up to leave out, follow me out because I'll be going into the bathroom to piss in the cup. I'll hand you the cup, do your thang and then hand it back to me. Understand," she explained.

Nodding I said, "Okay."

Everything was falling into place. My mother's attorney told her the drug test results will be ready in the afternoon, but not to leave the courthouse. So, we went into the cafeteria and ate lunch. Hours later we were back in the courtroom. Her name, well, all of her names were called. She had many aliases due to her constant arrests and two marriages.

The Judge happily announced that her urine was clean, per her probation order.

"And a congratulations are in order Ms. Sutton," the Judge continued, "Staying free of drugs is the best way to start off a pregnancy."

"Pregnant," my mother repeated with an unbelieving look on her face.

"Yes, you're pregnant. Be sure to make an appointment with your obstetrician to confirm. But congratulations again, you're free to go," the judge said.

My mother turned around and looked at me. I was sitting there in my mind saying *oh my God, she's not pregnant I am*!! I was fourteen years old, in the ninth grade, pregnant by a high school boy, no way I could possibly be pregnant.

"If you have sex and miss your period, you are pregnant," is what I heard echoing in the back of my head. It's what my mother always said to me and she had been declaring that exact statement to me for at least a year prior.

My mother had a lot of sayings, or what I would like to call *Wanda's Chronicles*!

So, we exited the court building and I met her at our earlier meeting spot across the street.

It Ain't All Jokes!

"LaWan, I cannot believe you are pregnant! Does Mike know," she asked.

"No," I answered shamefully.

"Hmm...I could use this information to get you back," my mother said in a plotting manner.

"Get me back? What do you mean get me back?"

"What the fuck do you think I mean? Get my daughter back. He's going to lose this case when I take him back to court," she stated as a matter of fact.

"But Ma, I don't want to live with you!"

"Well shit, he ain't no betta. You over there fuckin' and I bet you got pregnant in his house, didn't you? Huh? I know you did because he ain't watching you. Too busy chasing young girls," she stated heatedly.

We caught a taxicab to the strip. After exiting the taxicab, she called my Aunt Denise from a pay phone. She started crying real tears as if her heart was broken. I had never seen her so vulnerable before. She told Aunt Denise that I was pregnant and how it was my Daddy's fault. Aunt Denise decided she would be the one to inform my Daddy and they all agreed that I would have an abortion. I was never asked what I would like to do. My opinion about my body didn't matter. As far as they were concerned, I was a fourteen-year-old child, too young to be having a baby, period!

"How old is the baby's father," my mother asked.

"He's seventeen," I answered.

"Good," She answered. *"Never have sex with old men because they'll give you worms,"* is what she told me. Another one of her infamous chronicles.

We had a meeting with the boy. More like his life was threatened by my crazy mother and her goon friends. She told him the abortion would cost $300.00, which he gave me in a couple of days. My mother took the money from me, gave $50.00 to her friend Ms. Diane, who allowed us to use her DC Medicaid card so that I could have an abortion for free under Diane's daughter's name. Imagine laying on the hospital table, legs spread wide, and the doctor says, "Now Patricia, this will be a painful process, but you'll get through," knowing your name is "LaWan" but you can't correct him? Only illegal Wanda could pull something like that off!

As I stated earlier, my mother had a lot of sayings. Here are the ones I remember verbatim! Wanda said...

"Get as much money out of niggas before you fuck them. After they stick the pussy the dough will be less."

"Always make a dude tell you his real name, because if you have his baby you want it to have his last name for the birth certificate."

"Always carry a switchblade wherever you go. Cut a nigga in the throat and that'll kill 'em."

It Ain't All Jokes!

"Don't tell your girlfriends your business in the bedroom. They will go behind your back and fuck your man."

"Never go south on a man unless he eats your pussy first."

"Don't buy a man new shoes because he'll walk out of your life."

"Never trust light skinned women. They are sneaky!"

"White folks will never like or accept you."

"Make sure all your boyfriends are black. You can trust a nigga you know better than a nigga you don't know."

"Never have sex with a guy who attend your school or work on your job. If ya'll break up, you'll be distracted and have to see his stupid ass everyday with regret."

"Never be faithful to these niggas because they'll never be faithful to you."

"Never do drugs! Don't smoke, don't drink. If you do, your kids will hate you."

"A hard head makes a soft behind."

"Once a junkie, always a junkie."

"Always douche your pussy after each sex partner. You wanna smell good down there. One dude shouldn't smell the other dude on you."

"You're a fat girl, so you're built close. That's an advantage for you if you're gonna fuck these dudes out here. Soak in the bathtub with vinegar because it'll tighten your pussy walls."

"Deal with hustlers. Ain't nobody got time for a working nigga to get paid every two weeks. You need your money now."

"If a nigga hit you, come get me and I'm gonna kill 'em!"

"Never be the girl a boy cheat with. You be the girl a boy cheat on."

"Date dudes who are a few years older than you. Men are immature, so after you shave ten years off his age, that's how old he's going to act."

"Don't be no fool, stay in school."

"Whatever you do, don't get caught."

"Test your friendships. Tell a bitch a small secret of yours and see if she tells somebody. If she does, she ain't your friend. She's an associate."

"Never leave your friends around your man. The nigga can't give her a ride, her momma a ride, and he damn sure can't give her no money."

"Don't say once what you can't say twice. If you say something behind a person's back, be bold enough to say it in their face or don't say nothing at all."

"You will meet your match. Remember that!"

It Ain't All Jokes!

My mother said some of the craziest things I have ever heard in my life. It's amazing how I can quote her verbatim. Honestly, I've probably applied all of 8% of what she tried to instill in me. The other 92% just didn't make good sober sense and definitely not good godly sense. In her mind, I'm sure she thought she was really teaching me sound words to govern my life by.

LaWan A. Taylor Thompson

THE LATE 80's...OH MY!

The late eighties for me was a whirlwind of disappointments, craziness, unchartered territory, major mistakes, and the prayers of my grandmother and godmother availing much. Ninth grade I had a homeroom and English teacher named Mrs. Cleo White. That woman loved her students with an agape love. She was a stern teacher with perfect penmanship, and she motivated us to do our very best. I was always angry about one thing or another. I rarely smiled unless I was being the class clown, doing something fun, or doing what I desired to do which was nothing constructive for the most part. Towards the end of the school year each 9th grade homeroom teacher had to prepare their students for graduation, or what they officially called, Promotional Exercise. I had no desire to participate. I was still disappointed about the fact that I believed my mother would not be in attendance to support me or congratulate me and would probably show up to the ceremony high as a kite if she were to come. I experienced my mother's absence for my 6th grade Promotional Exercise, so I knew 9th grade would be no different. My mother exhibited no signs of a woman who loved and supported her children.

It Ain't All Jokes!

Mrs. White, in her own way understood me. We had a couple of candid conversations and she never judged me nor treated me differently than her other students.

Mrs. White handwrote me this beautiful letter, June 1986:

Dear LaWan:

You are a courageous and smart young lady. I have watched you grow and mature into a student who has the potential to go far beyond high school. Continue to love Jesus Christ. He will never leave neither forsake you. Shine bright and never let anyone steal your joy!

Love,

Mother White

I still have that letter to this day. That letter was my Bible and kept me encouraged for years to come. Many people counted me out, including my own mother and most of my teachers. Telling me I would never be anything in life. Telling me that I would ultimately drop out of school, become a teenaged mother, and strung out on drugs like my mother. Telling me if drugs didn't kill me the streets would. Sadly, most of the negative things that people said to me, I believed. I didn't have much hope within myself. Afterall, the DNA didn't fall far from the tree, and I was Wanda's daughter through and through. I looked like my Daddy, but I was most definitely Wanda's strong willed, disobedient child. Mrs. White's letter offered me comfort to see a glimmer of light at the end of my very hazy tunnel. I would read her letter every night before going to sleep. I carried it in my purse like a wallet, guarding it like I would my money. That letter saved me mentally.

• •

Washington, D.C., the Nation's Capital, where laws were passed, and where the President of the United States resides, was also known under the moniker as "Dodge City." It was an insane time to be living in D.C. where young black boys and girls were murdered daily. Each week I was attending at least two funerals of friends, classmates, and/or youngsters who lived in the neighborhood. It was sad, and all I could think about is I would be next. Unfortunately, I believed it.

It Ain't All Jokes!

I started living a very reckless and dangerous life. I stopped caring about myself and started feeling that no one else did either. Although my Daddy loved me, I felt he'd stop caring. Often, he would say, "I just wash my hands of the whole thing," which I interpreted as he didn't care. I felt he must've turned his back on me because all hope was seemingly lost. Let's face it, I was pretty much a handful to say the least.

Daddy met his wife while I was in junior high school. By high school, we had moved into her apartment. I surmised she'd never been very fond of me. I know I never liked her because I was a selfish child who purposely said things that caused my Daddy's girlfriends to exit his life indefinitely, which is probably why he had only introduced me to three. Children will ruin relationships if the foundation to which its founded is not strong. My stepmother had a daughter who was the exact same age as I was, we shared a bedroom. She treated me nice in the beginning, then the sister-relationship we started to build began to take a downward spiral. She didn't like my friends because as she put it, "they laughed at her," so I wasn't allowed to have company anymore. It seemed that my stepsister was granted every wish, while I was treated like the black sheep of the family. I started to hate them both and I told them such. When I would hang out late, my stepmother would lock the additional latch on the apartment door that I didn't have a key too, as a result I would sleep in the hallway of the apartment building. Remember, Dad worked the overnight shift 11pm-7am, so she would unlock the door at around 5:00am just as she was leaving out for work. I told my Daddy what she had been doing and he didn't believe me. There were a lot of negative things about me, but a liar was not one of them.

He said, "LaWan, if you bring your hind parts in this house at a decent hour you wouldn't have to worry about locked doors."

The thing was my curfew was being home before sunrise. I would get home around 4:00am if I bothered to come home at all.

My words one day to my stepmother was, "Bitch, I will set your ass on fire! Watch, after my Daddy goes to work, your ass is toast." Those words must've resonated in her heart because it was decided that living with my grandmother would be best for everyone.

I entered high school hating school altogether. Francis L. Cardozo Senior High School was pretty much a playground, but still I hated school. I wanted to run the streets with drug dealers and do nothing productive all day. I met a lot of fun people who came from other junior high schools, other than the school I once attended. It's amazing how a lot of my friends and I had a lot in common. In regards that a lot of them had mothers who were drug addicts. We didn't talk much about our issues. It was like an unspoken understanding that we all were in the same boat, except one friend I had. She and I took 10th grade Biology together. Class lasted roughly 45-50 minutes each day and we used the bulk of our class time talking about our problems. I would hear my mother's famous chronicle in the back of my head, *"what goes on in this house stays in this house,"* so I kept my home life problems to a minimum but let my friend lead the conversations as she did all of the chatting all of the time. I was a great listener for her and her stories, strangely, they were therapeutic for me.

One morning she whispered, "LaWan, has your mother ever sold you?"

Not knowing what she was talking about and looking at her skeptically, I answered, "Girl, no, what are you talking about?"

With tears in her eyes she explained, "My mother told me that I must have sex with the hustlers so that she could get her drugs for free. At least twice, sometimes three days a week."

I was shocked! I knew my mother was horrible, but in that moment, I remember almost feeling protected by my mother. Immediately I remember my mother telling me that one of the lead drug dealer lieutenants told her "for a night with LaWan, you can have whatever you want and won't have to work for it." She was a pathological liar, so I never believed her. But after hearing my friend share her sad story and god-awful dilemma, I believed my mother. I felt loved by my mother. For the first time my mother, unbeknownst to her, made me feel safe.

Nobody was better than another. The difference between me and the bulk of my friends was that I lived with my Daddy full time. That was unheard of in our community. As soon as someone discovered I lived with my father they'd ask, "Where is your mother?" My answer differed depending on the person. Some I may tell the truth only if they had a mother addicted to drugs or alcohol. If their mother was addiction free, then I'll say my mother was dead. Saying she was dead garnered positive attention. Meaning, they felt sorry for me and really pursued a genuine friendship. I couldn't handle the rejection of the truth, because I learned that people who had drug-free parents judged those who didn't. If I felt judged, I would fist fight them, which only made what they believed far worse.

My mother had been moving around the city a lot. Seems like every six to eight months she had a new address. I was living in a stable environment by this time, but I spent a lot of time at my mother's house in an effort to protect my sister. I was a master manipulator, so whenever my grandmother angered me, I would go and

It Ain't All Jokes!

stay a few days at my Dad's. When his wife or my stepsister acted as if I was the creator of bedbugs, I would go stay a few days at my mother's. When my mother started acting irrational, I would go back to grandmother's house and that cycle continued for about two years.

I loved Go-Go music and loved to party. When I was a little girl, Daddy introduced me to Go-Go music. Live bands like Experience Unlimited (EU), Chuck Brown & the Soul Searchers, and Rare Essence were my all-time favorites. All of my friends were "Go-Go heads" just like me. One Friday night I was getting ready for the Go-Go. I was 15 years old and I also had a part-time job working for McDonald's. My legs were shapely, toned, and void of cellulite so I loved to wear miniskirts. My grandmother didn't like that I attended events that were not church related. "Dancing with the Devil" is how she described clubs and parties. On this particular night, grandmother said, "Don't mess around and get yourself shot." Such a negative statement is what was running through my mind. I also thought my grandmother was jealous of me because I was young, full of fun and she was a boring church lady.

It seemed that I was my happiest at a Go-Go event or a party. Dancing was my favorite thing to do. I wore my hair in braids a lot, so sweating out my hairstyle wasn't a concern of mine. I arrived at the Go-Go around 10:00pm.

Rare Essence band was playing, and the lead male vocalist, Mr. James Funk, had such a captivating and fascinating speaking voice that was perfect for moving the crowd. He belted the lyrics through the microphone, "Put your Gucci watch on, synchronize the time and let's rock!" All the party goers went wild! The song that echoed those lyrics were a classic favorite. In a matter of moments, I hear a pop and see a flash. The guy standing next to me had been shot. I grabbed my stomach thinking I, too had been hit because of the impact of the fired shot which made my body vibrate. The guy fell to the ground and the crowd started running, screaming and many were trampled on. My grandmother's words resonated with me. Although I didn't get shot, it was as if I'd been warned. It was chilling. But it didn't alarm me enough to stay away from the street life. The life and the lifestyle were exciting and at this point in my life, I simply stopped caring about me and what could possibly occur to me if I didn't find a more positive path to follow.

    I spent a couple of weeks with my mother and sister. They were living in a D.C. shelter. It was an apartment style shelter for women in the transitional housing program. Still a shelter but, each family had their own apartment. There were many rules that accompanied living in transitional housing that many of the women loathed. It was the beginning of the year 1988, and the Washington Redskins was headed to the Superbowl. Good energy was all around Washington, D.C. On this particular morning, my mother was in the bathroom a little longer than usual. My sister needed to wash her face and brush her teeth before going to school. She came into the bedroom to tell me that Ma was still in the bathroom. I barged into the bathroom without knocking first only to find her sprawled out on the floor with a dope needle hanging from her groin. Blood was pouring from her vagina area and she wasn't moving. Seeing her like this was something I had grown used to. I was angry and hoped she was dead. My sister was more compassionate and very sympathetic than I. I hated our mother, but she didn't! I was strong as life hardened my heart. My sister was tenderhearted, sensitive, and full of optimistic hope.

I blocked my sister's view of our mother sprawled out on the bathroom floor appearing to be dead as a patch of brown grass.

I said to her in a firm tone, "Tia, don't look down. Step around me and go to the sink. Wash your face, brush your teeth, and don't look down as you leave, okay?"

Tia nodded her head up and down nervously. Visibly she was afraid.

As she washed her face and brushed her teeth, I made sure she focused on the necessary tasks and not on our mother's lifeless body. I made small talk in an effort to silence the dead air...pun intended. With the exception of the running water, all we heard was my voice. I helped her exit the bathroom and I shut the door behind us. My sister went into the bedroom we shared, and I went into our mother's bedroom and grabbed some money from her sweatpants pocket. There was no quick breakfast food in the kitchen, and we needed to eat. We left out of the building and walked a block east towards the Waffle Shop. We went inside, ordered breakfast and ate our meals in silence. I paid the waitress and left her a tip.

As we walked south down 14th Street heading to our respective schools, I told my sister, "Look, don't think about Ma. She'll be alright. She's always overdosing. But if she's dead, then she's dead. We are going to be better than her, okay?"

"Okay," she responded sadly.

I'm going to be frank my mother had been on my mind while in school. I pretended to act as if all was okay, but I was concerned. What if she was dead? Where would Tia go? Will Tia blame me because we left her, and I didn't call 9-1-1? So much was going through my mind that I was uncharacteristically quiet in my classes, which should be in The Guinness Book of World Recrods. Right before lunchtime, I was in my English class and the school secretary came through the loudspeaker. "Mr. Skehan, do you have LaWan Taylor in your class?"

"Yes I do."

"Please send her to the office."

Mr. Skehan gave me a hall pass so I could walk to the office without any problems. Indeed, I was problematic and stayed in trouble in and out of school, but this day I readily followed school protocol. I opened the office door and strolled in. Mrs. Johnson, the school Principal said to me, "Hi LaWan, please follow me to my office."

I shadowed Mrs. Johnson. When she opened the door, my mother was sitting in one of the three chairs that was across from Mrs. Johnson's desk. My heart dropped to the pit of my stomach when I saw her. My mother was staring at me stone faced. Her eyes were squinted in a wicked way and I knew she was conspiring her revenge.

"Have a seat," Mrs. Johnson urged.

Nervously I took a seat, intentionally in the chair furthest from my mother. My mother was an excellent street fighter, swift with her punches, and would swing without warning. I made certain not to be within striking distance. I was 16 years old, in excellent shape, and I was swift on my feet. Much quicker than her, yet, my brain admonished *don't sit next to Wanda*.

Mrs. Johnson start speaking. My mother interrupted her and turned to me asking in a calm voice "Were you going to leave me for dead, LaWan?"

I didn't answer. Mrs. Johnson resumed her speech. Again, she was interrupted with, "LaWan, do you hate me that much that you'd leave your own mother on the floor for dead? At least you could've called 9-1-1. But you tell Tia how tired you are of me and if I'm dead, then it'll be a weight off y'all shoulders. You really hate me, don't you LaWan?"

In my mind I was thinking, *dag, she heard me in the bathroom. She wasn't dead, just her usual passed out.*

My mother started rising from the chair slowly. I jumped up from my chair hurriedly. "May I go back to class, please, Mrs. Johnson," I asked in a rushed tone.

"Yes, you may, LaWan."

I exited that office rapidly. In my heart I was relieved she wasn't dead and at the same time wished she wasn't living. I just didn't want to be named the individual responsible for her death. After school I went to my Daddy's house.

February 26, 1988, I turned 17 years old. My Daddy gave me money and a birthday cake. I was given money and presents by the guys I was dating as well as the hustlers. Surprisingly, my mother called me and said she had a gift for me. She had given me money and a birthday

It Ain't All Jokes!

card. A very cute birthday card with a picture of a little girl on the front walking in the rain holding an umbrella, which I've kept to this day. What intrigued me the most about the card was the way my mother signed it.

"You are my best friend and one helluva daughter."

Love Ya,

Wanda

She didn't sign it "Mom" like most mothers would. I presume this was out of her element since she'd never given me a birthday card in the past.

March 1, 1988, my mother had another court date. She was facing up to 13 years in prison. Selling illegal drugs was her hustle of choice, therefore she experienced many arrests and had to pay a hefty consequence. Per usual I was to take her urine test for her. I knew the routine, as I have done it for her for the past 3 years. Her attorney was a beautiful woman who I grew very fond of. Often, she and I would talk over the phone whenever I had inquiries about my mother's pending cases. She never knew my urine was being used for the drug test, at least I wasn't naive to share that with her during our open conversations.

Once the judge freed my mother, I remember her attorney advising firmly but with a hint of sisterly love, "Stay out of trouble Wanda."

She then turned to me, "LaWan, I'm putting you in charge of your mother. Keep her out of trouble. The next phone call I expect to receive is the one that says she is staying on the straight and narrow path."

My mother and I were all smiles which I believed were genuine, at least for me it was. We hugged her attorney, said our "thank you's" then exited the court building. We walked two blocks away to hail a taxicab. Inside the cab I gave my mother back her belongings she asked me to hold in case she would've been detained. Her money, cigarettes, door key, and pocket size address book. Usually she carries a switchblade with her, but it would've been confiscated upon entrance into the courthouse. We got out of the cab on the corner of 14th & W Streets, NW. It was roughly 2:20pm so I knew going to school would've been a waste since school ended at 3:00pm. My mother gave me my "pay" for my clean urine, so I headed in the direction of a friend's house whom I scheduled a hair braiding appointment, days prior. She walked towards Ms. Peggy's house to go shoot up.

It Ain't All Jokes!

I was sitting on the chair while my friend was standing next to me braiding my hair. It was still daylight outside when my Daddy and sister came to the apartment of my friend. When they walked in my sister was crying. Immediately I thought she had been in a fistfight resulting in her loss. It was odd to see my Dad appear, but then again, he was always the supporter, so showing up was in his nature. I was irritated that Tia wouldn't stop the tears and hollering.

I screamed at her, "Tia, shut up! What are you crying for? Whoever hit you I'll knock them out once she finishes my hair!"

"Ma died," Tia said sadly as tears rolled down her face.

"LaWan, your mother passed away a few hours ago," my Daddy said in disbelief. I remember seeing the concerned look on his face and hearing the empathy in his voice.

My friend who was braiding my hair, dropped the comb and started screaming, "Oh my God, not Aunt Wanda! No, not Aunt Wanda!"

"Girl, if you don't stop all that crying Tia. She didn't care about us so I'm glad she is dead," I spit from the heart.

Turning to my friend angrily, who was crying in hysterics, I said "girl, you need to finish my hair, shoot!"

"LaWan, are you okay," my Dad asked sympathetically.

"Yes, Daddy! My mother didn't care about us, so now she's dead and we won't have to worry about being called b's anymore," I answered visibly irritated and furious!

My mother was found dead in the alley behind Ms. Peggy's house, with a dope needle handing from her groin. She died of an overdose. Isn't it ironic that someone tossed her into the alley to die, the exact way she tossed Petey into the alley? Undeniably, we reap what we sow. Karma is real.

My mother didn't have any life insurance, so I asked every hustler who helped put the dope in her veins for money for her burial. I collected close to $9,000, but she was buried for free. D.C Government covered all the costs. My mother was buried March 7, 1988. Sadly, no family members on my mother's side offered to become Tia's caretaker, who was 12 years old, except for our Aunt Denise. Her biological father wasn't in her life, so essentially, my mother was all she had to depend on. My Daddy and his wife volunteered to take Tia in temporarily until our aunt's apartment was ready. She lived with them almost two years.

It Ain't All Jokes!

Traditionally, African American Washingtonians celebrate Easter Monday by attending the National Zoo. It was a tradition that derived from Blacks being barred from the White House Easter Egg Roll. This year, 1988, hundreds of us decided we would go to Kings Dominion instead. We all dressed in expensive matching Sergio Techini sweat suits and Reebok classics. I borrowed my Aunt Linda's Subaru and five of us including my sister piled into the small hunter green sedan. Initially, we were having fun. We were standing in the line for the *Grizzly* rollercoaster. A lady decided she'd cut in front of my sister in the line. I told the lady she could not cut the line. Ignoring me, she remained in place. I snapped and grabbed the woman by her long, flowing, dark hair and began to beat her face. The next thing I knew two police officers were dragging me through a wooded area towards the amusement park's ranger station. As a result of my public use of profanity I was arrested and barred from Kings Dominion for ten years.

Summertime came and I was living an extremely reckless, dangerous, risky, crazy, and out of control life. Hanging with the wrong people, befriending individuals who didn't embody anything positive, and not loving myself or others. D.C.'s "Mayor for Life," Marion Barry, kicked off an initiative, D.C. Summer Youth Employment Program (SYEP) which allowed D.C. youth ages 14-21 to obtain a job working during the summer. In addition to working for SYEP, I worked at People's Drug Store, and sold street pharmaceuticals. After all, sitting under the tutelage of my mother, I learned the drug game well. I linked up with a New Yorker who was a DC drug supplier. I never knew his government name, just his nickname. In my mind, since we weren't romantically involved, knowing his name was unnecessary. He was a very nice guy to me, but ruthless and coldhearted to many others. He was a strategic thinker and was serious-minded about making money. He expressed to me he wanted to be a millionaire and retire out of the game. I had major respect for him. Hired as a driver, my job was to transport drugs from New York to DC. He said he wanted a female with a valid driver's license to drive because the likelihood of state troopers pulling a woman over on the highway was very rare. I believed him so I agreed to be his driver.

In the beginning transporting drugs from New York to D.C. was scary. He provided a brand new 1988 Nissan Stanza, equipped with a nice radio and cassette player, leather seats, and a car phone that didn't work. After a few successful transports without incident, I felt super confident with my new title. Earning $1,000 per trip, that was good tax-free cash for a 17-year-old girl. He didn't need me daily, but often enough, and I was excited to hit the road.

As a result of living the street life, I was raped. The guy who raped me was a popular guy and we knew each other. He'd already raped a few girls prior to, but I didn't believe he would violate me.

Some friends and I were in the Arcade playing Ms. Pac Man. He came in and whispered, "You're going with me."

I remember laughing! I mean, laughing a good hearty laugh because I thought he was kidding. As I continued to play the game, he came up behind me and squeezed the back of my neck and said, "Let's go!"

It was chilling, and in that moment, reality started to set in. Afraid to say anything because of his ruthlessness, I walked against my will towards the front door. He hailed a cab and we hopped in. I'm holding my purse thinking, *"LaWan, pull your scalpel out!"* But instead, I decided to put my hand on the door handle. With the quickness of a panther, he backhanded me across my face and said, "Don't try it." I was literally seeing stars as tears fell from my eyes. Shocked and stunned with fear, I felt paralyzed. The taxicab pulled in front of a shabby looking apartment building in Northeast, DC. We exited the vehicle and I stood there on the sidewalk. Why didn't I run? Why didn't I run? Why didn't I just run? To this day, I don't know why I didn't take off running for my life. I just stood there. Stoic! He grabbed the back of my neck and said, "Come on." We walked into the stale smelling apartment building and into a unit on the ground floor.

He began to make small talk as I remained silent standing in one spot.

I remember asking him, "Why me?"

He smirked and said, "Take your clothes off."

After the rape concluded, weirdly, he gave me $40.00. I took the money and put it in my pocket. He called a taxicab for me. When the taxi arrived, we both exited the apartment. He opened the back door and said, "Don't tell nobody or I will put a bullet in your head." I hopped in the backseat. Giving the driver a ten-dollar bill, he told him to take me wherever I wanted to go. Home to my Daddy's house is where I went, and I never told a soul. At least not immediately.

School resumed and I decided I didn't want to attend Cardozo anymore. With special permission Daddy transferred me to Spingarn High School. Quickly realizing Spingarn was not a good choice because I had a lot of enemies who attended that school. Each day my life was threatened by groups of girls from a rivalry neighborhood.

It Ain't All Jokes!

I wasn't afraid of them. Females didn't evoke any fear in my heart. Getting jumped by a mob of angry females is what I tried to avoid. Towards the end of the school day, each day I would use the office phone to page my boyfriend to pick me up. Two months of threats and one unfair fight was enough to tell Daddy I need to return to Cardozo.

I hated school. I like working legal or illegal. Working and making money were my goals, not obtaining an education. After my mother died, I still wanted to become a police officer, but the passion to become one was slowly dissipating.

••

"Hello?"

"Good Morning, my I speak to LaWan Taylor, please?"

"This is LaWan."

The nurse on the other end identified herself then asked me to confirm my birthday and medical record number. Then she asked if I preferred to come into the office for the results or give her verbal permission for the results over the phone. I agreed to listen right away.

She started sharing and when I heard, "You're pregnant", afterwards her voice sounded like chalk scratching on a board. No way, I could be pregnant. The IUD was removed only a few months prior, so no way I could be with child that quickly. *Who's the father* I asked myself as I tried to calculate dates on the calendar?

No adult in my family expressed happiness for me. I was 18 years old, officially dropped out of high school and working a low-wage job as a cashier. Living in my grandmother's home, unwed, no education and no money saved, she was visibly upset.

"LaWan, you can't bring no baby in this house with no husband. I didn't allow your Daddy to bring you in here, and you are not bringing one in here either."

"So, what are you saying, grandmother," I asked.

"No babies can live here. Is that boy gonna marry you?"

"You were unwed when you had both my Daddy and Uncle Tee, so why are you judging me? Y'all church people are all the same," was my disrespectful response.

"Start looking for a place to live, LaWan! You can't bring no baby up in here," she said with finality.

I stopped working at McDonald's. Not because I was fired, I was stressed trying to find a permanent place to call home, so I eventually stopped going to work.

It Ain't All Jokes!

To add insult to my already pitiful pregnant state, in a matter of a few short weeks, I became homeless. To my knowledge no friends knew. They believed I was just angry with my grandmother and refused to go home. I started spending nights with various friends if their parents would allow. On nights when permission wasn't given, or if my "potential baby daddy" didn't call me back, I was left with no options but to sleep on the streets. In my mind, I had an image to uphold, so I would walk around all night instead of sleeping on the actual street. When the sun rose, I would board the local bus and ride for hours in hopes of getting sleep. I had clothes at the homes of friends, my grandmother's, my Daddy's and aunt's, so I would go by either places, shower, eat and change clothes. Again, no one knew I was technically homeless as my unborn baby continued to grow. I remember one night a pimp approached me asking if I needed a place to stay. No, was my quick response. Prostitution wasn't my thing.

The guy who I told was the father of the unborn gave me money all the time. He was a drug dealer, and in my mind, he was my boyfriend, although being exclusive was never discussed. I would use that money for food and clothes, but not for shelter. Young, ignorant and idiotic was the best way to describe my mental state.

In my heart I knew I had no business bringing an innocent baby into the world. I wanted better for the baby and felt I couldn't provide it. Not wanting to be a mother like the one I had, I boldly placed a phone call to an adoption agency. It was one of the hardest phone calls to date. After making the appointment and visiting the counselors at the adoption agency, I didn't feel relief, but a wise decision had been made.

About six months into my pregnancy, living like a nomad was taking a major toll on me physically. I was losing weight which concerned the doctor during prenatal visits. I used the payphone to page my New York connect. Since I no longer had a stable home to live in, waiting by a landline for his phone call proved to be impossible. He called back and I was transparent with him about my home situation. As luck would have it, he had a dope house that needed a worker. He preferred that I transport instead, but while I was homeless, the dope house would be a perfect fit for my dreadful situation. He carefully explained the pros and cons of drug dealing from a dope house. At this point in my life, I didn't see no easier way out. Again, having a mother as a drug dealer, living in a dope house was going to be as easy as a toddler learning their ABC's. Included in my drug dealing benefit package, I would have direct access to money and to the Nissan

Stanza that I missed terribly. The dope house's one-bedroom apartment was fully furnished and smelled nice. I smiled when New York and I walked in. It was home…for now. Ironically, the building was located directly across the street from the building where I was raped. How weird is that? Putting what happened to me out of my mind, I concentrated on the task at hand, which was making money.

    Drug sales at the dope house was doing quite well. Customers knocked on the door all day and all night. Crack cocaine was in high demand in the black community. I was there alone, and New York came by every so often to collect money and to bring food, beverages, and more supply. Things were going almost perfect for the first six weeks. I started picking up proper baby weight in accordance to the prenatal chart module at my doctor's office. I felt happy from the inside out!

    One evening a regular customer came by twice that day. All of the customers were addicted to crack cocaine, but, this certain guy was always polite and not very talkative like most addicts, but seemed concerned because he'd ask questions like "How's the baby," or "How many months are you now," so I liked him. Unproblematic are the customers salespeople hope for. On the third time of his visit, he knocked on the door. I watched out the peep hole, saw it was him and opened the door. My usual routine for regulars. He walked in behind me and another guy came in from behind him and put a gun to my head. The gunman was not visible when I looked out of the peephole.

"Give me the motherfuckin dope and money, bitch!"

"Oh my God," I yelled out in a stunned semi-scream.

"Where the money at? Where the drugs at? I'll shoot yo pregnant ass, think I'm playing? Huh? Huh," he said in an intimidating voice as he held the gun aiming it directly at my skull.

I heard my grandmother's words so clearly as if she was in the dope house with us, *"If you call on Jesus, He will answer."*

Dropping to my knees, I prayed out loud, "In the name of Jesus, don't let him shoot me!" I repeated that statement several times and would not stop saying it. I believed my grandmother's words and I begged the Lord Jesus Christ hoping he would move on my behalf. NOW!

"Fuck that Jesus Christ shit! Where's the shit girl? You think I'mma motherfuckin' joke, huh?"

While the gunman was threatening me, my favorite customer was rummaging through the neat apartment until he came across money and a drug stash. He also dug

It Ain't All Jokes!

his dirty hands in my navy colored sweatpants and stole the $118.00 I had in my pocket.

"I found it. I got it Joe, let's go," favorite customer said to his partner in crime. They immediately left.

I was shaking so badly I urinated in my comfortable Gap sweatpants. My stomach kept fluttering and I thought I might lose the baby. I got up from my bended knees and locked the three bolts on the wooden door. I was terrified and could not stop myself from trembling. I've seen people pull out guns, I've ran during drive-by's, I've seen individuals shoot others, but none of that prepared me for having a gun shoved in my face. I paged New York, entering the emergency code 9-1-1 after entering the call back number. He called back immediately, and I told him what happened. He was out of town and advised me to remain inside the apartment until his return, which was three days later. For three days I never opened the door. People knocked all day and all night. The addiction to crack was real. And I wouldn't answer the door. The television was turned on but the volume was muted. I stayed up all night and took naps during the day. I was almost afraid to breath for fear that my favorite customer and his partner in crime would return.

Drug dealing and the dangers thereof was not for yours truly. That incident taught me two things. One; that a fast life of crime equates to being buried six feet under.

And two; if you call on Jesus He will answer. Up until that point my life wasn't much to be proud of, and I was a very miserable young lady, but I didn't want it to end at the hands of a robbery gone wrong.

Back to the drawing board I restarted my quest to find a new place to live. New York offered another dope house to sell from or resume transporting product from state to state so making money could continue for both of us. For fear of my life and the life of my unborn, I told New York I was out of the game. He was understanding and said if I ever needed work, he was just a page away.

I had roughly a little over $2,000 in my designer purse and more maternity clothes that any pregnant woman could ever need, with no residence to call home. I started making phone calls. People were nice and begin to allow me to live with them, which was short lived. Interpersonal skills were horrible so living under the roof of others was proven to be exceptionally difficult for me. In other words, I couldn't get along. I didn't like rules and I hated being told what to do. Within two months I had lived with three different families. Life was already tough, and my rebellion made things more challenging than necessary. My mother said, *A hard head makes a soft behind*, and I could feel the pain of her statement almost every day.

It Ain't All Jokes!

At 8 months pregnant, I started living with my Dad's ex-girlfriend. I chose not to like her while they were dating and made fondness of me almost impossible. Yet, she was nice, kindhearted and sincere despite my actions. A woman with a heart of gold. She had a husband, two sons, and was currently pregnant with their only daughter when they opened their home to me and my unborn. They lived in a quaint, exceptionally clean 2-bedroom apartment. I shared a room with their two sons.

September 20, 1989, 12:49am, my precious daughter was born, weighing 7lbs, 4oz. She was soooo pretty! Perfect! Angelic! Innocent! A gift from God! I just stared at her in awe. I could not believe I had a beautiful daughter. No way I could be a mother! Holding her I introduced myself, "Hi Courtney, I'm your mother, LaWan. I don't know what I am doing having a baby at 18 years old, but you're here now. I love you and I will be the best mother that I can. As long as you obey me, we will get along just fine."

A friend from the neighborhood told me that if I apply for welfare, the social worker will help me obtain affordable housing. There was hope! At this point I needed my own home so no one would have the authority to kick me out. I called the adoption agency the day I gave birth and told them I'd had a change of heart. I was keeping my baby and give this thing called motherhood a shot. Although I wasn't raised by a good mother, I drew from the fact that I can do the exact opposite of what Wanda did and raise my daughter In a loving way.

Leaving the hospital three days later with an infant baby girl, I started making plans to find permanent housing, a car, employment, a babysitter, and a good boyfriend. Maybe not in that order, but those were on my important list of attainable goals.

I slept on a twin bed and my daughter slept in her basinet. Courtney was a very good baby. She didn't cry for the first 25 days of her life. She would suck her thumb, smile and look around. Undeniably a blessing! My fear was that if my baby cried, then I would be requested to move out expeditiously. However, Dad's ex didn't seem to mind, as she encouraged and helped me to adjust to motherhood. It wasn't easy at all. A mother's job is the toughest on the planet. I wasn't obligated to give her rent money, but I was responsible for providing my own food for myself and my baby. That was a first and strange experience for me. All the other families I lived with, I had to pay at least $50.00 per week and I slept on couches or on the carpeted floor.

I applied for many apartments that accepted DC Government Housing vouchers and income-based apartments. Most had a 2-3 year wait list. Oh my goodness, I needed housing now. Dad's ex was an amazing woman, but I believed my eviction was coming soon since residing with people never worked in my favor. Three months later, I can't recall what happened with her husband's job, but he no longer had one. She was a stay-at-home wife/mother with no stream of income, totally dependent upon him. As a result, bills were unpaid, the electricity was disconnected, and they had received an eviction notice from the leasing office. Winter was in full effect and the only reason the apartment wasn't cold was because she turned on the oven to warm up the unit. But it was very dark when the sun set. I told her that I would begin searching for another place to live and she understood. She was a Christian woman and prayed God's choicest blessings for my life. My heart was touched.

    I made some phone calls and as luck would have it, a woman who is like an aunt to me opened her home to us. For the first time, Courtney and I had our own bedroom. My monthly rent was $290.00, and my monthly welfare check was $329.00. Yikes! Anxiety was getting the best of my emotions as my mind said, *page New York*. I had to keep that old life in my rearview mirror. Instead I called the many companies that I applied for jobs to see if my applications were received. A blessing came when I was hired at Hecht's warehouse! I made enough for rent and had an amazing babysitter, Ms. Verdie. I love Ms.

Verdie! She's the kind of woman who everyone trusted with their children and your child was always safe and well fed. Still to this day, she holds a special place in my heart. Working, taking excellent care of my infant baby girl, and staying out of trouble was just what the doctor ordered. Life was beginning to show me a little grace and happiness.

    My Daddy came by to visit us at his play sister's. I don't how a casual conversation took a left turn, but we started arguing. It was a very bad argument to the point that Daddy was so close in my face I could smell his hot breath. I said some very threatening things as my play Aunt begin to join in on the argument telling me if I'm going to disrespect my father then I would have to move out. Furiously, I told her I would leave at the end of the month since I paid my portion of the rent. Walking into the bedroom, slamming the door, I wanted to cry but was too livid to let a tear fall. It was sad enough he chose to believe the voice of that evil wife of his, and I can't live with him, now he was on the other side of town picking fights with me which resulted in me needing a new place to live...again! I felt this was not my fault.

    Three weeks later baby girl and I were moving out. My God-sister said we could come and stay with her. She had one son and lived in a one-bedroom apartment. Courtney and I shared the couch. Things were going well between us. We got along fine. We were a lot alike. She was a few years older, but I admired her and had a great deal of respect for her. A couple of months of living there, I saw a medium-sized rat! Yes, an actual rat. Not a barely there house mouse, but a rat. I was scared to death of rats, mice, and any creature in the rodent family. The rats seemed extremely joyous, playing at night, running from the kitchen to living room and back to the kitchen for hours on end, as if I purchased tickets to a circus. After a couple of sleepless nights, out of fear for my baby and I being bitten, I had to find another place to live. I was sad but living with rats was not an option for myself and daughter. Well, at least I wasn't receiving another eviction. I was proud of me!

    Spending nights with friends, motel and hotel stays were draining and unstable, I was tired and needed permanent relief. I remained friends and in constant contact with Dad's ex. She allowed me to use her address and phone number when applying for jobs and employment. The seasonal job I had ended, and I was broke and homeless again. I had been periodically attending my grandmother's church, the one I grew up in, but I stopped feeling comfortable there. I felt so judged by the members. So, when Dad's ex invited me to her church I accepted. I felt no one would know me personally and I'd be able to cry in peace.

Sunday, April 16, 1990, I attended her church, Abundant Life Faith Bible Church in Takoma Park, Maryland. There were lots of younger people there and the church was loud with praise. You could feel such a delightful and joyous energy in the room. At that time, I couldn't discern the presence of God or knew what it felt like, but I realized what touched my soul was so unfamiliar, yet loving, warm, inviting, and without judgment. It was surprising to see that two friends I had since before junior high school were members. The sermon was a typical Easter sermon. Nothing said stuck with me, but I remember being mesmerized by the pastor's use of the Bible. It was my first experience hearing a female preach.

"Is there one," was the question that Pastor Shirley Nicholson asked the congregation at the conclusion of her sermon. This was the "Altar Call."

With compassion in her voice, Pastor Nicholson continued, "Is there one who wants to give their life to the Lord. God told me you're here. You've been weary, unsure, and have tried everything except God. Why not give Him a try today? He loves you! He gave His only begotten son, Jesus Christ, to die on the cross for your sins. Will you accept Him into your heart today? Is there one?"

It Ain't All Jokes!

As tears cascaded down my cheeks, I whispered to Yolanda Strother and said with sincerity, "I'm going down there."

"I'll hold the baby," she offered.

"No, I'm taking her with me. She's all I have."

I stepped from my seat and walked down to the front of the church where Pastor Nicholson and the Intercessory Ministry team members were in place to receive those who wanted to give their heart to Jesus Christ. Holding Courtney tight, my face drenched with tears. A new chapter had begun. I was saved! God is good! Hallelujah!

After repeating the sinner's prayer, the members rejoiced with singing, praises to God and many gave me hugs and encouraging words. I believe I felt different, but I can't honestly say…maybe because after 30 years of being a Christian I am changed now, but I know there was a transformation because I didn't want church to end. I wanted to stay there, in that loving place forever.

Dad's ex cooked dinner and invited Courtney and I to spend the night. That was a relief. I was so caught up in the move of God, that for a long moment, I forgot about my homeless reality.

Dad's ex said, "LaWan, something good is going to happen to you. God is going to bless you beyond your imagination."

"Thank you. I hope I get a call from the apartment complex because we need someplace to live," was my hopeful response.

"I know the leasing office said an apartment won't be available for another year or two, but I believe God is going to open a door for you, because the Bible says the last shall be first and first shall be last," Dad's ex said with faithful conviction.

Monday morning the telephone rang around 8:30am. I think Dad's ex was in the shower or something because I answered the phone.

"Uh, yes, may I speak with LaWan Taylor please?"

"This is LaWan."

"This is Mrs. Waddy at the Parkway Overlook Apartments. We have a one-bedroom available and your name is next on the list. Do you still have one child?"

"Yes ma'am," I said excitedly, hands trembling, heart pounding, a nervous energy brewing on the inside of me.

"Okay great. We need to schedule a home visit. This is done for every applicant. Are you still residing at 2907 Stanton Road, S.E., #204," Mrs. Waddy asked.

"Yes," I lied. That was Dad's ex's address, that I was using for professional purposes. I did live there for a short time, then spent the night last night, so as far as the application was concerned, I lived there.

It Ain't All Jokes!

"Okay great. Is 11:00am today good for you?"

"Yes, it is."

"Okay, I'll see you at eleven."

When Dad's ex appeared, I told her about the conversation. She immediately started praising God! She was screaming, "THANK YOU JESUS, THANK YOU JESUS!" She was doing what Christians call *praising God in advance*. I hadn't got the blessing officially, but she was activating her faith with an advanced praise.

Inspection ended up being a housing interview, which went exceptionally well. So well that I moved into my FIRST apartment April 20, 1990. Four days after I had given my heart to Jesus. I couldn't believe it! I could not stop saying, Thank you Lord!" I couldn't stop smiling! I could not stop crying tears of joy! I could not stop thanking Dad's ex for being the blessing she remained. God was good just like they said He was. He moved me at the top of the waitlist. I was in amazement. No more getting put out onto the streets. Finally, I was going to be stable. I think if Courtney could've comprehended that moment, in baby babble, she would've rejoiced as well. *"The first shall be last the last shall be first"* became my official favorite scripture! God truly answer prayer.

SATAN'S COUSIN...MY EX-HUSBAND

I had been living on Robinson Place for three months. Attending Sunday services each week along with Bible study, I was happy. Quickly becoming a member of Abundant Life Faith Bible Church, I felt it was a great decision as it related to my spiritual growth. God removed all the troublesome friends that weren't good for my spiritual, physical and mental growth. No bridges were burnt, I just stopped visiting them, they stopped calling me as life continued to move forward. Still not owning a car, my Dad's ex picked me up for church each week, which I was eternally grateful.

■■■

"Yes, may I have a Bomb Pop and an ice cream sandwich, please," I said to the owner of the ice cream truck as I pulled out my dollars to pay for my purchases.

"You live around here," a man behind me asked.

"Yep," I answered.

"What's your name?"

It Ain't All Jokes!

"LaWan."

"My name's Dino."

"What's your real name," I asked.

"James. You got a boyfriend?"

Smiling widely and proud, I answered, "Jesus!"

His wide smile matched mine and he responded, "Oh yeah! Jesus is my boyfriend too."

Instantly I thought I'd met another Christian who would help me pray for this crime-ridden neighborhood that we lived in. I wasn't attracted to him romantically, but we exchanged telephone numbers, which you'll see was the absolute worst decision of my life.

We started dating immediately because he said, "You know you're my girl, right?" I was blushing and nodding in agreement.

July 5, 1990, my grandmother died. She laid down to take a nap and never woke up. I remember many times walking into her bedroom throughout the years only to hear her praying, "Lord, I wanna live to see LaWan change." And she did!

August 1990, I received a happy phone call from Temple Court Apartments in N.W. Remember, I had applied to many apartment buildings while homeless and it seemed that my favorite scripture was working on my behalf. I didn't like Southeast DC, so I happily accepted the two-bedroom apartment in Northwest.

Along with that news, I learned that I was pregnant. Yep, pregnant with my second child. I wasn't super excited about the news, because I didn't want any more children since I was struggling to care for the one I had. Here I was a babe in Christ, learning scriptures, Bible stories, attending church at least twice weekly, but was pregnant with no husband. James was excited! He had two children prior, but he didn't seem to mind having another.

I moved into the 2-bedroom apartment immediately and months later he moved in with us. As my stomach grew, my pregnancy became extremely difficult. I was spotting a lot and some days there was heavy bleeding. My doctor put me on bedrest. I visited a church with a woman named Zee. The pastor of the church was a Prophet. I've never met or even heard of her prior to visiting with Zee. She pointed at me and asked me to come down to the front. I obeyed. She prophesied to me saying, "God said you're carrying a difficult baby boy. There's bleeding and discomfort daily. God said, the baby is breach but he's turning the baby. Before you deliver the baby will turn and this miracle will shock the doctors." Tears just flowed down my face and I truly believed she was sent as the mouthpiece of God.

My due date was April 25th and this baby showed no signs of wanting to meet his family. The doctor said due to the baby being breach, a cesarean would be safest.

It Ain't All Jokes!

I could hear the prophet's words in back of my head as doubt began to creep in. I was scheduled to have the cesarean April 27th. The day had come. Dad and James accompanied me which I was glad I was not alone. I knew all too well what that felt like and it wasn't nothing good to boast. My water had broken on our way to the hospital. Labor officially begun! Hours later, I still hadn't dilated, but the contractions were strong. A sonogram was prearranged when I first arrived, and baby was still breached. At this point doubt had covered my brain. I didn't have faith in this area, like I had for the apartment.

"LaWan, you've been in labor now over 15 hours, so we're going to prep you for cesarean delivery," the head Labor & Delivery nurse said.

"Okay, but can I make a phone call first, please?"

"Sure. I'll call for the Anesthesiologist and your doctor, who'll meet us in the cesarean room. Hang in there," she was soothing and encouraging.

I was in a LOT of pain. If you're ever had a toothache, labor pains are ten times worse! I called my godmother because I knew she would pray. Over the phone she began to speak God's word and call His promise to His remembrance. We hung up and I was wheeled into the cesarean room. As the Anesthesiologist attempted to help me sit up, I said, "It feels like I need to push." In one push, my baby boy came out HEADFIRST just like God said he would! 7:30pm, weighing 8lbs 4ozs, Kendall Isaiah Hight entered the world. A handsome, healthy son! Who looked just like me. I was pleased!

■■

The guilt of shacking was taking its toll on my spiritual growth, so I told James it was best that he moved out. I didn't want to end the relationship permanently, but a righteous choice had to be made. He understood and moved out for about two months.

"LaWan, let's get married. I love you, you love me, so we might as well make this family thing official," was his proposal.

"Okay," I responded as I leaped from the couch excitedly to retrieve the calendar. Getting married was a great idea as I felt he was my soulmate. We had a good relationship, he loved Courtney and now we had a son together. Yep, we were destined to be.

Selecting August 31, 1991 as our wedding date, we were broke. I mean, super broke. My ring was given to him from a woman that used to date his Dad. She had a lot of nice jewelry and let him have the ring for free. I purchased his ring from a jewelry store for $69.99. Three easy payments later, I had the ring in my possession. We begin announcing our engagement to anyone who would listen. The church friends I had made at Abundant Life were extremely supportive and happy for us. We didn't have a wedding planner as such, my church friends started planning the wedding and so many people made donations. My wedding dress and shoes were a loan, the bridesmaids dresses were made by Tonita Majors, a skillful seamstress costing them $10 each, volunteers cooked the food, and Uncle Willie made our scrumptiously beautiful wedding cake. James rented his tuxedo and his groomsmen wore the ugliest and most uncoordinated shirts that didn't match the pastel theme we selected. In other words, they looked a mess.

    My former friend Zee was not happy for us at all. She called me two weeks before the wedding and said, "LaWan, God said don't marry him. James is not the man for you. Let God save him first, clean up his heart and then marry him. But if you do, you'll regret it." In my heart, I believed her, but I didn't share what she said with nobody. I wanted what I wanted, and that was to be Mrs. James E. Hight, III.

    Siblings Kenny Lattimore and Trinnita Lattimore sung a beautiful song at our wedding, "Lord, make us one." As they sang in sync, James and I held hands at the altar lovingly. I was 20 years old; he was 25, and I should've run for the hills.

"And I now pronounce you husband and wife. You may kiss your bride," Pastor Nicholson jubilantly said. We kissed and our family and friends cheered. It was a beautiful wedding, a talkative reception, I was happy, he was happy, and we were in marital bliss for about 45 hours.

"Bitch, I don't wanna hear that shit," my brand-new husband said to me two days after our wedding. I could not believe he called me a bitch. He had snapped with such a rage that caused me to cry. I was thinking, *LaWan, you just married Satan's cousin.* Although no one was around, I was inwardly embarrassed. I felt I made a huge mistake marrying this guy and wished I had listened to Zee. I needed God to save my husband.

Every day we argued. We couldn't seem to communicate effectively. It's funny how we were master communicators while shacking up, but as soon as I decided to do what I thought was right, all hell breaks loose.

Six weeks after saying our *I do's* I was sitting on the toilet seat crying. I was miserable and my stomach had been cramping terribly. The pain intensified and I felt something fall from my vagina and drop in the toilet. I knew it wasn't a bowel movement but possibly my cycle started since it was overdue. I looked in the toilet at what appeared to be a fetus. Immediately I knew I'd miscarried. In that instant, it was a blessing because this household was too toxic to add another baby.

    Early November I was sorting dirty clothes to prepare for the laundry. I was always a secure woman, so I never searched my husband's clothes looking for evidence of other women. I will assume he's faithful until there's proof that he's not, but I'm not going on an amateur detective hunt looking for confirmation. He had all types of things in his pockets per usual, which was no big deal. A piece of white paper was folded so small that it almost looked like lint, caught my eye. My heart dropped as intuition kicked in. Taking deep breaths trying to calm my nerves as butterflies brewed in the pit of my gut, I unraveled the tiny piece of paper. A wife's worst nightmare…another woman's telephone number! Her name and number were written in I'm assuming her handwriting with the words, "Call me," and she added a lipstick stained kiss on the paper. A mixture of anger and hurt flooded my body. He was cheating on me. Not even three whole months into the marriage and he was cheating on me!

    Courtney was running around the apartment and Kendall was in his baby seat. James was in the bedroom asleep. I was standing in the living room, dirty clothes placed in piles according to darks, lights, and whites. I was trying my hardest to remain calm. The more I looked at the note from Miss Ruby Red, the more enraged I became. So what did I do? Rushed into the bedroom to confront his cheating butt. I shook him awake and started screaming accusations. As he was gathering his bearings, he got up from the bed and started denying he was cheating. I demanded that he call little Miss Ruby Red right this minute to prove to me that he wasn't cheating but he refused, which infuriated me. I then told him to get out now, to which he responded he's not going anywhere. I threatened him then stormed out of our bedroom. Going into the kitchen, I picked up the telephone and called the police. He followed me into the kitchen as we resumed arguing.

Two uniformed African American officers knocked on the door. James went into the bathroom and I let the officers in. Still very angry I was huffing & puffing, out of breath, talking extremely loud, using every profane word as I told them in a nutshell, "Get him out of my house now, Officer!"

Officer Arthur and his partner walked to the bathroom door and asked James to come out. He said, "Man, she is crazy as hell. Threatening to kill me, so I'm not coming out unless yall protect me from her dizzy ass."

I walked into the kitchen, placed a pot of water on the stove and walked back out. Oh, I was planning to get him good. He let the Christ in me fool him, thinking I was a soft, frail punk. I was still Wanda's daughter and vengeance is mine, not God's. He would leave here, but not before he felt the hot wrath of my fury. Finally, the officers convinced him to open the door and nicely asked him if he would leave the apartment for at least 24 hours so I could cool off. He agreed, walking into the bedroom for what I believe were his shoes, and coat. Moments later he started walking down the hallway with the officers in tow. I stepped backed into the kitchen, in a flash I had the pot of boiling water in my hand. I said, "Fuck you, you cheating ass bastard," then tossed the pot of hot boiling water. Missed him totally as hot water landed on Officer Arthur and his partner. DAMN! Out of the apartment I went... in handcuffs!

Back together we were after the $25.00 Disturbing the Peace fine was paid. The dysfunction continued.

A week after the hot water disaster, we were arguing again. It got really bad, because I suspected he was still being unfaithful. We both were screaming at each other, name calling, and degrading one another as best we could. I started to get the better of him in the argument as I attacked his manhood and his ability to financially support me as his wife. I was still receiving a welfare check, food stamps and had a husband. Berating him as best I could, I most definitely was the winner of the argument.

Then he stepped close in my face and said, "Keep talking shit and Imma fuck you up in here!"

"Your bitch ass ain't gon' do shit to me. Where the fuck yo ass gon' live? Huh nigga. I met your gutta ass at a ice cream truck with no shoes on your feet, living with your sister and no job! Bitch ass nigga you need me. You ain't shit without me. You can't eat without me. If I don't buy the soap, your uncircumcised dick won't get washed, so you betta shut the fuck up," I spewed venomously.

"BITCH," he shouted and with one punch he hit me and I dropped to the floor.

Yes, he knocked me out cold. When I came too, there was three unfamiliar men around me, including James. I felt a clicking inside of my jaw, so I put my left hand on my face. It hurt as I tried to talk. One of the three men identified himself and the others as Emergency Medical Technicians (EMT's) who were called to help me. James was sweating, looked worried, and kept whispering in my ear, "LaWan, I'm sorry baby. I'm sorry!" In my heart of hearts I knew I would exact revenge. The police arrived and begin to ask me questions. I didn't want James locked up because I wanted to execute my personal revenge, so I lied to the policemen about what happened.

It Ain't All Jokes!

The ambulance took me to Howard University Hospital. They took x-rays, blood, and urine. Results were in. My jaw was broken, and I was a month pregnant. This dude was hitting me with sperm and punches all in one. I remained in the hospital for four days. My mouth was wired shut!

With only being able to drink liquids and foods as soft and thin as baby food, that was my diet for eight weeks. I remember 2-year-old inquisitive Courtney asking questions like, "What's that on your teeth?" "Mommy, say ah." "DeeDee why is mommy talking like that?" (DeeDee is the name she called James) Kendall was 7 months old, so I started giving him table food because I needed his baby food for myself. I also remember not having anything to eat Thanksgiving and Christmas 1991. I drank the liquids from the greens, chitterlings, and drank lots of egg nog. I was more so sad and embarrassed rather than mad. New Year's Eve 1991, I was sitting in Bible Way church crying. Trying to worship and praise God though I felt He couldn't hear my voice through a wired, closed mouth. Entering the new year 1992, jaw wired, down 32 pounds, pregnant, miserable, marriage has totally fallen apart and I started praying, "Lord, please save my husband."

July 3, 1992, I woke up that morning with my nightgown and panties drenched in blood. I heard the voice of the Lord say, "Get to the hospital now. The baby will come quick and you don't want to have him at home." Initially I doubted the voice was that of God's. I wasn't due for 15 days, plus I'd already given birth to two children prior, so I felt maybe something else caused the bleeding. Not the baby is coming. I called James at work and told him about the blood and what the Lord spoke to me. Laughing he said, "Yeah, yeah, yeah, you're always talking about what God said. Look I'll meet you at the hospital." Pissed with his non-supportive attitude, I slammed the phone down. I called Mrs. Dolly and asked her for a ride. Mrs. Dolly was the grandmother of the friend that braided my hair the day my mother died. Mrs. Dolly was a praying woman who loved family and would always extend herself to others, especially in the community. She was loved and respected by all. Mrs. Dolly agreed to pick me up saying she'll arrive in thirty minutes, so I got myself, Courtney, and Kendall dressed. I gave them both bowls of cereal. I didn't eat anything because if I was in labor, I didn't want to vomit. Before going downstairs in the lobby of the apartment building to wait for Mrs. Dolly, I called James back.

"Hello, this is James," he answered the phone at his place of employment.

"James, Mrs. Dolly is picking us up and taking me to the hospital. Make sure you come because I have Courtney and Kendall with me."

It Ain't All Jokes!

"Man, why you got Mrs. Dolly picking you up? She smokes cigarettes and I don't want her smoking around my kids," he said with a slight attitude.

"If your ass stop drinking and running around with these women that don't want your ass, maybe you can buy a car so your wife won't be calling others for rides," I snapped.

"Man, shit, I don't wanna hear that. Why didn't you call your father?"

"Because he didn't get me pregnant. What the fuck? Look, be at the hospital dumb ass." I screamed and slammed the phone on the receiver.

Mrs. Dolly dropped us off at Providence Hospital. She offered to take Courtney and Kendall off my hands, but I told her James was on his way. She prayed for me, gave me a hug and we exited her vehicle. The nurses were kind and kept Courtney and Kendall at the nurse's station with them. After changing from my sundress to a hospital gown, I called James to let him know I'd arrived safely at the hospital. I also called my father and a few friends. Talking on the phone with one of my fun friends for about an hour, *The Price is Right* was just going off on the television. All of sudden my water broke. Pain hit me instantly and intense. I hung up the phone immediately as I rang the bell for the nurse. Labor had officially begun.

LaWan A. Taylor Thompson

At 1:18pm, Kenard Isaac Hight came into the world, three weeks early, weighing 7lbs. 11ozs., and 20 inches long. The most quickest labor I've ever had. No epidural was needed. He popped right out. He was so pretty he could pass for a girl. He was so soft, fluffy and kissable that I instantly nicknamed him "Fat Baby."

James showed up to the hospital roughly 3 hours after Fat-baby's birth. I was pissed that he missed it.

"What's up boo," he said when he walked into my hospital room. Looking at my now semi-flat tummy, he says, "Damn, you had the baby that quick?"

"I told your stupid ass God said the baby was gonna come quickly. Keep on thinking God don't talk to me, hear? I had a boy, I named him Kenard Isaac Hight. He's down the hall getting circumcised and having his first pictures taken. Go to the nurses station and get Courtney and Kendall and tell the nurses thank you for keeping them." I almost said in one breath.

In a huff he responded, "I know to say thank you, but let me go see my little man first."

The next day the baby and I were released from the hospital. Not even twenty-four hours after giving birth, the doctor said I well enough to be discharged. I was prepared to leave, I felt great and was craving crabs anyway. Since I'd just gave birth, I thought it would be inappropriate for me to attend the 4th of July cookout at

Aunt Linda's house, so my daddy bought crabs to the house for me.

A week after Fat-Baby was born, James called me from work crying. His only daughter had been fatally hit by a car and died on the scene. Janelle was seven years old. I prayed with him on the phone. I'd never experienced that kind of lost before so I couldn't imagine his pain. He kept screaming, "WHY GOD WHY! PLEASE DON'T TAKE MY SONS FROM ME!"

The night before the funeral, he said he wanted to stay at his Aunt Penny's home, and I understood. He said, "LaWan, I need you and my kids with me tomorrow. I promise you I'm going to change, be a better husband and father. Please don't give up on me, please." I was moved emotionally, and I believed every word he said. After all, I asked God to save him, so however the Lord chose to answer prayer, I'll be satisfied.

Courtney, Kendall, Fat-Baby and I showed up at the mid-sized church for the funeral, which was super packed. I started hugging family members as I looked for James. We spotted each other and immediately he grabbed the baby seat from me with Fat-Baby still inside as he grabbed Kendall's hand.

Then whispering he said, "We're gonna sit up near the front, but you can sit towards the back just in case Courtney gotta go the bathroom."

"What do you mean I can sit towards the back? I'm your wife! I'm sitting with you," I said through clenched teeth trying to remain unruffled.

I followed them down to the second row, but I felt myself seething so I chose to sit on the third row behind him instead. There was a woman sitting directly beside him that I'd never seen before. I tried to tell myself that she was a family member I'd never met because family members from all generations attend funerals. But this woman was too contented with him, and not in a bloodline way. As he started crying during the program, she slid closer and wrapped her left arm around him. I'm staring at them from behind. One of his male cousins walked down the aisle and said something to her, which I can't remember, but when he said her name, my heart dropped. It was Miss Ruby Red! He'd had the audacity to have his side bitch at his daughter's funeral with his wife! What the hell?! *He's still fucking her* is all I kept hearing in my brain. I wanted to punch them both in the face. I stood up, grabbed the baby seat with Fat-Baby in it and placed it on the bench in between me and Courtney.

Then I snatched Kendall off her lap, and whispered to them both, "I should fuck both of y'all up in here."

Turning to her I said in her left ear, "Bitch, don't ever put your hands on my children again. And you will die of cancer of the uterus for sleeping with a man who's married to a woman of God." She sat docile! James was about to say something to me but couldn't fast enough as I marched swiftly with my three children towards the exit.

■■

Providence Hospital is a Catholic Hospital, so practicing methods of birth control is against their beliefs. I made an appointment to have a tubal ligation done at Columbia Hospital for Women. The appointment was made two months after I gave birth to Fat-Baby. I arrived at the appointment only to find out that I needed my husband's written permission in order to have the procedure. I felt frustrated. Accepting the paperwork from the nurse practitioner, I made an appointment to come back in a few weeks.

Initially James was opposed to signing the paperwork. We argued and I told him, "If you don't sign it, I will forge your name. You just want to keep me pregnant so you can keep me under your control. But no more babies will come into this house. But you can always go have one with that fat face trick you had at the funeral." He signed the paperwork.

After dropping my three children off with my Dad the morning of my appointment, I eagerly arrived very early. The appointment was a waste of my time. It was a mental prep counseling session of sorts, to ensure that each woman is acutely cognizant that tubal ligation is an irreversible surgical procedure that after it's done, will become unable to conceive again. I was the only woman in the room smiling from ear-to-ear. I didn't care if they said tubal ligation would cause hair loss, anal warts, and discoloration of the urine, I was GETTING MY TUBES TIED! Another appointment was made for November, which was prearranged to be the actual procedure. James was supposed to keep the kids, but he didn't come home the night before per usual. I called Dad and asked if he could keep the kids while I attend this must-make appointment. Dad agreed and came over immediately to pick up the kids. I took public transportation to the appointment and made it in time. They took blood and urine as I sat in the pre-op room patiently waiting. A member of the medical surgical staff came in with a weird look on his face. He started asking me how I was feeling and things of that nature.

"Mrs. Hight all of your tests results came back and you're healthy as a horse. However, you are pregnant."

My jaw dropped as sadness consumed me.

"Well, you can get dressed Mrs. Hight...," he began his spill.

It Ain't All Jokes!

Mentally I checked out. He sounded like Charlie Brown's mother. All I heard was *wah, wah, wah, wah...*

After putting back on my clothes, I exited the building. I was steaming mad! I sat on the Metrobus letting angry tears fall. I wouldn't talk to God. I remained mute. When I picked up my children, I told my Dad the appointment had to be rescheduled. He didn't ask any additional questions. I packed up my children and went home.

James didn't come home that night. James didn't come home the next night. Twenty-three days later, James still hadn't come home. I asked the manager in the rental office to change the locks and to remove his name from my lease. At this point rent was due, phone bill due, Fat-Baby needed pampers, and the household was lacking overall.

After the maintenance guy changed the locks, the kids and I boarded the Metrobus towards the Department of Human Services building, with my new lease in the baby's bag, I needed emergency assistance. Mr. McPherson, my social worker was a soft spoken and sharply dressed man. He expedited finances and food stamps for me which allowed me to pay the rent, phone bill, purchase diapers, and everything else we needed within 24 hours.

Sitting in the living room watching a television program, I heard keys jingling outside of my apartment door. James! He was trying to insert his non-working key in the lock. Realizing it wouldn't fit, he knocked on the door.

Sauntering to the door, I nicely asked, "Who is it?"

"LaWan, it's me, open the door."

"The locks have been changed because you moved out, so get the fuck away from my door," I responded matter-of-factly.

"LaWan, please open the door. Look, I'm sorry. Please open the door and let me explain," he begged.

"Slide the rent money, pamper money, and phone bill money under the door and you can come in." There was a long pause from him.

"Damn, LaWan, you got folks all in my business, just open the door, damn."

"Slide the rent money, pamper money, and phone bill money under the door and you can come in." I repeated with a little more base and volume.

"Mannnn, you one materialistic bitch," he snapped!

"Materialistic? Nigga, if I was materialistic, I wouldn't be with yo' broke ass!"

He started kicking the door. I threatened to call the police and after a few more kicks, he left. Walking back over to the couch to finish watching TV, I told my innocent babies, "Y'all daddy dumb as dish water!"

Days, weeks, and months were filled with going to church, prenatal appointments, kids birthday parties, a periodic movie, visits to the playground, grocery store, and arguing with that mistake I married almost every day.

August 7, 1993, three days after my due date, I woke up knowing I was in labor. I was experiencing mild contractions the night before while at church, but I didn't immediately leave for the hospital. After birthing three babies, I believed I was proficient in child delivery and pretty much only needed a willing participant to cut the umbilical cord.

I called my God-sister Crystal for a ride to Columbia Hospital for Women. Kent Immanuel Hight came into the world weighing 9lbs even and 23 inches long. There was no room left for me to carry him because his feet were often underneath my rib cage. A very uncomfortable pregnancy towards the end although a smooth one void of complications and restrictions. He looked just like his Daddy. I couldn't find me nowhere. A handsome and strong tyke that I loved at first sight. He was born at 12:45pm, and my tubes were tied an hour later. YES, FINALLY NO MORE PREGNANCIES! For those of you who love babies and desire a plethora of them, a round of applause goes to you. On the 4th day God created the sun, moon, and the stars. My 4th child completed the family just as God completed the universe.

About a month or so later I had a hair appointment on the other side of town. James was at one of his sister's apartments and asked if I would stop by so we could ride back home together...on the Metrobus. I agreed. After my hair was done, I stopped by. When I walked in there was a cute little infant boy on the couch. He was so adorable that I hurried over to where he was laying and scooped him up into my arms. I begin to kiss on the cute stranger and talked to him in a baby-like tone.

"Whose precious baby boy is this," I asked while smiling down at baby adorable.

"Oh...I don't know. My sister's babysitting and I think he belongs to her friend that lives downstairs," he answered.

"Oh cool."

I changed the baby's diaper, fed him, burped him, prayed over him and just held him. He looked familiar and I kept thinking I may know at least one of his parents. He was content, which reminded me of our son Kent, who was his exact age.

Some weeks later I was on my knees at 12noon praying. I wanted to attend Bible Way's noon-day prayer service, but the kids all fell asleep. The Bible says, "Where two or three are gathered together in the spirit, He's in the

It Ain't All Jokes!

midst," so I figured while I'm praying at home 12 noon which is the same time as the intercessors at Bible Way, God would meet all of our requests. I was on my knees in prayer for about two hours. As I rose from my knees the telephone rang and answered.

"Praise the Lord," I greeted the caller joyously.

"Hello, may I speak to a LaWan," the female caller asked.

"This is LaWan," I answered cheerfully. After all I'd just rose from my knees deep in prayer.

"Uh, are you LaWan Hight? Married to James Hight?"

"Yes I am. Who is this, please," I asked politely.

"Oh my God. You do exist," she said sounding astonished. "Well, your husband has a baby by my daughter. Somebody said his wife was a church lady and so I looked your name up in the phone book."

My heart had totally left my chest cavity all together. I was shocked almost into silence. In an instant, I saw the face of baby adorable whom I held just weeks earlier. The grandmother was talking, but I zoned out. All I felt was the blatant betrayal from this bastard I said *I do* too.

Cutting her off I said, "I saw the baby. I held the baby. I changed the baby. I fed the baby. I prayed over the baby." Tears started cascading down my make-up free cheeks.

To add salt on my wound she said, "It sounds like you met my grandson, Kendrick."

"Kendrick...Kendrick...Kendrick," I repeated.

She started talking but my brain was trying to comprehend it all. *Why would God set me up like that? Why did this nigga give that baby our "K" name that was our family's signature? Why did he let me hold my stepson as if he was the neighbor's child? OMG me and his adulteress was pregnant at the same time! He's really out here slinging that short dick around as if it's the best thing since sliced bread. I really married SATAN'S COUSIN!!*

Cutting her off again, but a little more curtly I said, "Thank you for calling and sharing. Your daughter will more than likely end up with cancer of the uterus for sleeping with a man who's married to a woman of God. Please don't call here again and if you do, I won't be this nice."

After abruptly hanging up from the baby's grandmother, I walked into our bedroom and started bagging up all his clothes, shoes, toothbrush, toiletries, personal business papers into large black garbage bags. I dragged the bags down the hallway and tossed everything he owned in the trash chute. I was so sick and tired of his infidelity. It was high time I started demonstrating that I was not to be taken for granted anymore.

Ms. Annette, the Assistant Manager in the rental office called me one morning. "Hi, Mrs. Hight. This is Ms. Annette in the rental office. Your name has been selected to receive a 4-bedroom townhouse. Are you interested?"

"Huh? Wait, what? I…I…I didn't apply for a 4-bedroom townhouse I actually applied for the 3-bedroom apartment," I honestly corrected while attempting to process what she said.

The volume in her voice dropped down to an almost whisper as she said, "Mrs. Hight, I know this. But I want you to have it. Many of these young girls in this building are so disrespectful, destructive and ghetto but you are different. I'm not giving them the house over you. So miss lady agree to accept and come see me to sign the paperwork."

"The first shall be last and the last shall be first," my favorite scripture came to my mind. I was so elated I called everybody to share my blessed news. One of my Bible Way friends said, "What you experienced my dear is the favor of God. Pray for his favor always and you'll see more doors will open for you than you've ever dreamed of." *Favor…favor…favor…*I locked that word in my head and my heart to use and never let it go! FAVOR!

I'd forgiven James again. Taken him back...again. He promised he wasn't going to cheat or disrespect our marriage...again. I was still holding on to hope that God will change him and believed he would change this time...again! Our marriage was still as toxic, emotionally, physically abusive as ever.

Moving day had arrived! I was so excited I couldn't stop smiling and talking about the goodness of the Lord. James and I both asked male friends to assist us with the move. Four of my guys including my Daddy and five of James' guys showed up. Moving from a 2-bedroom apartment into a 4-bedroom townhouse was going to be fairly speedily with eleven strong men. Pretty much everybody arrived at the same time, introductions were made, and I was preparing to give directives.

"Hey LaWan...let me holla at you in the back," James said.

We walked into the now packed bedroom.

"Who are those dudes? I'm sayin'...I ain't never met those dudes before and they just show up out of the sky. Are you fucking any of them," he asked in an accusatory tone.

With a deep sigh, I paused and answered, "No!"

"You lying like shit! Dude in the gray sweater was watching yo ass. I know you fucked dude!" He snapped.

It Ain't All Jokes!

"Dude in the gray sweater is married. He does not want me or no other woman for that matter. He loves his wife, which I am friends with her too. If your ass went to church, you would've met both of them by now," I said livid.

"Nah fuck that! Let them niggas move you," He said matter-of-factly.

He stormed out of the bedroom and down the short hallway to the living room. He picked up his one box marked *James,* says to his friends, "Come on y'all, we out!" They followed him and left. *All things work together for the good to them who love God and to those who are the called according to His purpose* is what the Bible says. The world says, *one monkey don't stop no show.* James leaving and taking his crew didn't stop us. We moved into my new low-income townhouse in the hood! I smiled happily and thanked God.

∙∙∙

For months James had been calling me asking if we could get back together. I learned he fathered another baby, this time a daughter, and with the same baby's mother. SMH! This dude simply did not love me at all and cared even less about the sanctity of marriage. He started visiting the kids regularly which they enjoyed.

One evening he came over drunk. The heavy smell of alcohol reeked through his pores. A voice spoke to me saying, "*You're going to jail tonight.*" Out loud I whispered, "The Devil is a liar," speaking into the atmosphere a rebuke that would counter the voice I heard. I wasn't receiving nothing absurd and random in my spirit. James was acting weird and I wanted him to leave, so I started ignoring him. I didn't want to argue because my friend Pam was at my house. Busying myself, I started cleaning up. 8:00pm was approaching so I drew bath water for the two youngest toddlers. He came in the bathroom and started asking me random questions about my sex life. Ignoring him still. He left out of the bathroom and I heard something break, so I ran from the bathroom into my bedroom as he was knocking things off my dresser. I called out to Pam asking her to look after the kids. She was on the third floor; my bedroom was on the second.

"James, you need to leave."

"Why, so you can fuck some nigga," he said as he started ripping up pictures of our family. I tried to stop him, but he turned around swiftly, pushing me. I didn't fall but hurried down the stairs as he came chasing after me. Into the kitchen I ran and pulled out a butcher's knife from its holder on the countertop. We stared at each other.

It Ain't All Jokes!

"Satan, I command you to leave this house now! You have no authority here. Leave Devil."

Smirking like a possessed demon, James said, "Make me bitch!"

Looking him directly in his eyes, with zero fear I said, "James, if you don't leave, you will meet the Devil you serve face-to-face. Tonight, will be the night you leave Earth."

"You must be scared, bitch. You got that fucking knife in your hand. Scared ass bitch. That's why I had a daughter cause your fat ass couldn't give me one and I will love my other kids better than I love yours bitch. That's why I be fuckin bitches in your house when you at church. Yous a stupid bitch."

I stood in place with the confidence of a bear, never taking my eyes off him. He got eerily quiet. A voice spoke to me and said, "*He's going to lunge at you.*" Nodding my head slowly, I was ready for his attack. My mother taught me how to use knives and scalpels with precision, therefore he was venturing in the wrong lane.

Moments later he charged me trying to pry my fingers from around the knife.

"Yeah bitch, yeah bitch, you gonna give me this motherfuckin' knife. I'mma kill your ass," is what he was saying.

LaWan A. Taylor Thompson

Using my left hand, I grabbed another butcher's knife from the holder on the counter and swung it, which swiftly chopped off his right ear.

Screaming in agony like the weak excuse for a man that he was, I was slicing him every which way with both knives. He stumbled from the kitchen, begging for his life, bawling, crawling, and yelling for help, into the living. Showing no mercy, I screamed, "I TOLD YOU TO LEAVE SATAN!" Both hands swinging, not caring where the knives landed. Three of his fingers were cut off as well. Permanent cuts across his head, giving his haircut new meaning.

Pam obviously called the police, because I heard a cop say, "Police freeze! Put the knives down now, ma'am." I looked up and both cops had their guns drawn on me. Dropping both knives immediately, I then lifted my hands high as I started worshipping and praising God! Blood was everywhere, James was on the bloody floor squealing like a wounded raccoon, and I was giving God all the glory saying things like, "Thank you Jesus I won't be leaving on a stretcher," "Thank you that I won," "Thank you that I am free!" I was smiling, relieved, and unafraid. For the first time in my marriage, I felt a mental shift, and I asked God sincerely, "Help me to be strong enough to release James from my heart and my life. I want out of this marriage by divorce if he lives." Many cops came into my home and a few I knew personally which worked in my favor. So instead of handcuffing me and placing me under arrest, I was allowed to stand off to the side where I was pushed when I dropped both knives until I was to be transported to First District police station. Thank God Pam was there, because the kids would've been taken into Child Protective Services.

One curious officer said to me, "Ma'am, what if your husband dies? You could go to prison for life. You seem like a church lady so tell me why you stabbed your husband."

Still on my Holy Ghost high, with the widest smile ever, I said, "David had a rock and a slingshot and slew the Philistine giant, Moses had a rod and parted the Red Sea, and I had two knives. Whatever you find in your hands to do, do it with all of your might!" Officer Curious stared at me as if I should go to a mental institution instead of jail.

Leaving my house in loose fitting handcuffs, James on a stretcher, I was glad it was not the other way around. A large crowd was gathered around my house and I heard somebody say, "Damn, the *praise the Lord lady* killed her husband." That rumor still exists to this day.

When I arrived at the precinct there were messages from friends who called to see if I was okay. Pam called everybody. Before placing me in the cell, the nice officer showed me the messages on the pink While You

Were Out message pad. As she was talking, I looked across the glass and spotted my Daddy. He came to the precinct to see about me. Daddy! Always my BIGGEST supporter! Tears sprang up in my eyes as I confessed to God, "I don't want to be here. I don't deserve this. I want to go home."

My night in Central Cellblock wasn't as bad as I thought. Being that I knew some of the cops personally, they allowed me to sit in the area with the officers instead of my cell. *FAVOR!* I had two huge donuts and a large cup of orange punch which had a lot of sugar. At around 4am, I had to be placed in a cell. All inmates and those arrested was to be arraigned starting at 8am.

The cell was filthy. There were so many roaches that was unrecognizable. I had never seen a roach with wings, that had eyes like a fly, but moved faster than a mouse. And there was many. I wouldn't sit on the metal bed, so I remained standing to keep those floaches (fly-roaches) from crawling on me. I was placed in a cell with a prostitute, who'd be arrested for prostitution. She had large pasties covering her nipples, booty shorts that barely covered any of her booty, 7-inch-high heels stripper shoes, and many sores on her lips. Cute face minus the herpes and she was very young.

She said to me, "You look like a nice lady. Why are you here?"

It Ain't All Jokes!

"I am a nice lady. I love Jesus and I don't belong here," I responded with a humble smile.

With squinty eyes and a curious look, she asked, "So, tell me what happened to Adam and Eve in the Garden? I mean…was Adam cheating on Eve and then God kicked him out. What was up with them?"

I was soooo elated she asked. I was enrolled in Calvary Bible Institute in my first year, so I was able to teach her everything I knew from the book of Genesis to Revelation. I talked from roughly 4am until we were transported to the courtroom hours later. Miss Prostitute was inquisitive and if she's alive today, I pray she's doing well for herself.

The Judge released me on my own recognizance with a promise to return for the pre-trial hearing. I was happy to be released. I left the courtroom with my Daddy, and he drove me home. I wanted to see my children, take a long hot shower, and get some much-needed sleep. At this point I'd been awake for over 29 hours. Pam was a doll with a heart of love. She cleaned up ALL the blood, disinfected the floors, the kitchen, and had my home looking better than new. Such a friend and I'll forever be grateful to her for that.

Yolanda came over to my house and sat with me. She listened and offered comforting words. She cried as I had to laugh to keep myself from crying. Many friends called to check in on me and I was appreciative. A few of James' cousins called threatening to "whoop my ass." I told them, "if you have the number, then you have the address so come thru." I was never scared, and they never came.

Oh...and my ex-husband lived and recovered well in the hospital. When he was released, he called, and I refused to speak with him. I had no words. *"LaWan, if you weren't born with him, you can live without him,"* are the encouraging words I told myself. Freedom in my mind had begun...I was OUT!

PEACE, BLESSINGS, RESTORATION...

With my tubes permanently tied, Courtney & Kendall in school, Kent's potty-trained and attending daycare with Fat-Fat full time, I desperately needed and wanted a job. I applied for McDonald's and I was hired. I was excited because it was a start. Sometimes we must crawl before we walk. I didn't earn enough to discontinue food stamps and Medicaid, but the monthly check was replaced by my gainful employment check.

After a year of working at McDonald's I purchased my first used car. A 1987 Chevy Nova. I took the kids to Ocean City for our first family vacation. Life was looking good, feeling amazing, and was going exceptionally great for me.

I petitioned God for a lot in addition to a car, I wanted a career, and a home that belonged to me, not the government. I wanted my children to attend Calvary Christian Academy and I wanted us to travel.

I stumbled upon an opportunity to work for a sales company. I can't remember the name, but I was hired, and the starting salary was $21,000 per year. I immediately left McDonald's as I was moving on to bigger and better opportunities. I arrived at the new job prompt and professionally dressed. There were at least thirty other new hires as well, so I found that to be fairly odd. A gentleman came into the large conference room, introduced himself and explained the nature of the business and expectations of what our jobs would entail. While he was speaking, I quickly surmised, this was not a legitimate company but a scam. *Oh boy, I made a mistake leaving McDonald's* is what I thought to myself. When the guy gave us a 30 minutes break I hopped in the Nova and left.

After dropping the kids off at school the next day, I drove to McDonald's and asked for my job back.

"Sorry, LaWan, but we're not hiring," is what the Manager said to me.

"Huh? I was just working here three days ago, so how is McDonald's not hiring," I asked in disbelief.

"Your position has been filled."

I couldn't believe my ears. "It's McDonald's! Yall are always hiring."

"Sorry," was his final response.

It Ain't All Jokes!

I know what I asked God for and so I wasn't going to worry and neither was I returning to welfare either. I'd learned a lot about exercising my faith and that's exactly what I was determined to do. No going backwards. Forward thinking. Forward mindset.

Saturday morning after dropping the kids off at Dad's, I went to my hair appointment with my stylist Sher'ri Williams at Open Door Hair Gallery. I was sharing with her the bizarre week I had. My voice is naturally loud and it's the kind of loud that "carries" when I talk. A woman named Tonya Gray was in the beautician's chair across the room from me but heard everything I was saying to Sher'ri.

"Excuse me, my name is Tonya Gray and I couldn't help but hear your conversation. I am a manager at a staffing agency and if you wouldn't mind, send me your resumé Monday morning, I think we have a receptionist position that's brand new and I believe you'll be a good fit."

"Would it be okay if I bring my resumé directly to you," I asked hopeful.

"Sure," she answered and gave me her business address.

Monday, May 20, 1997, I arrived at the Staffing Agency dressed casual in tan khaki pant, a chocolate colored long sleeve shirt with black loafers. I was professional looking enough and Tonya was gracious when she told me my outfit was perfectly fine. She explained President Bill Clinton announced an initiative to partner with businesses throughout the country to employ welfare recipients. The Welfare to Work Partnership (WTWP) was launched as a result and was headed by Mr. Eli Segal, CEO. They needed a receptionist and who would be a better candidate than a former welfare recipient herself?!

I started the next day as a temp, which turned permanent six months later. My very first office job. I was an excellent typist averaging 120 words per minute, with beginner's knowledge of computers. I met some fantastic people at WTWP. Lisa Dawe taught me a lot about working in an office setting and helped me enhance my computer skills. She wasn't my immediate supervisor, but she was the person that made me feel extremely comfortable as I asked her many questions in a quest to grow. I was a fast and eager learner, who soaked up information and applied where necessary. Sherril Stone was my lunch partner turned lifetime friend! Sherril is few years younger than I but had a drive to obtain her career goals which fueled me inwardly. Overall, I loved working there and felt I was a perfect fit.

      One summer day, 1998, I got home and received letters in the mail from The Washington Scholarship Fund congratulating me on receiving partial scholarships for Courtney, Kendall, and Fat-Fat to attend Calvary Christian Academy (CCA). I shouted for joy! HALLELUJAH! God answered my prayer! Faith without works is dead. I remember when I applied for the scholarships, laid hands on the application before submitting and prayed, *"Father God it is my desire that you bless my children to attend Calvary Christian Academy. FAVOR this application as you've done for me in the past. You said in Your Word that whatsoever I ask in Jesus' name, it shall be granted unto me. I am asking in the name that is above every name, In Jesus name I pray, Amen."* My babies were going to attend private school. Kent didn't receive a scholarship that year because he was entering kindergarten. Nevertheless, I enrolled him in CCA with his siblings anyhow. Bishop

Alfred A. Owens, Jr., who was my Pastor at the time, called me and offered to cover the cost of his book fees, which was a blessing. I was eternally grateful.

    I was afforded the opportunity to travel to Chicago, Illinois for our Welfare to Work Partnership anniversary. My children traveled along with Aunt Denise. It was my children's first time flying on an airplane and it was an incredible experience. Except, Kent, who was deathly afraid of airplanes. The WTWP Conference was nothing short of successful. We stayed in Chicago five fun days. Well, it was a fun vacation for the kids and Aunt Denise, but a lot of hard work for me. The highlight for me was meeting, shaking the hand of former President Bill Clinton, and taking a group photo with him. I will never forget that awe-inspiring moment.

    A week after returning to work, I was called into Joanne's office. She was my direct supervisor. Joanne started talking casually and then told me, "Sorry LaWan, but we're going to have to let you go. You are being terminated, effective immediately." I was shocked! How could they hire a welfare recipient, have them travel with them to an event to *"show off"* the great example they were to other businesses, yet terminate my employment without just cause. Holding back tears, I left her office, walked to the receptionist desk, gathered my personal things and I left immediately. My only friend in the office, Sherril, was home on maternity leave, so I called her at home and shared. She offered to be a professional reference if I needed one, which I appreciated.

One would think worry would set in. Nope! I was flowing in a spirit of peace and God was restoring me. I was NOT going to worry, my children would remain in private school, I wouldn't lose not one single thing I worked hard and honestly to obtain. I never drank alcohol, smoked, tried drugs or any other self-destructive habits so I wasn't going to start now. I was going to fight the devil tooth and nail. If nothing else I was a survivor and I've overcame many obstacles with the Lord's help. I encouraged myself by speaking these words over my life, *"LaWan, if you weren't born with that job, you can live without it!"* As a self-motivator, I started creating all kinds of new mottos to live by. They work for me.

Job hunting became my number one priority. After dropping off the children at school, I drove to the unemployment center and started an intense job search. I faxed my resumé to several companies. Self-driven, self-determined, prayerful, strong-minded, and resilient best described my mindset. When I arrived home that evening there was a voicemail from Eli Segal asking if I could return his phone call, so we can discuss my future. My future?? Was this guy kidding me?? I never returned his phone call. Forward moving and forward thinking was my mindset. No going back! No going back!

The kids had a field trip, so I happily accompanied them as a chaperone. Mr. Bernard Perry, Principal of CCA noticed how well I interacted with the students and offered me a job as a teacher's assistant. I happily accepted.

During the Christmas season the staff of CCA was preparing for our annual Christmas celebration and Gong Show. Having always been humorous, I decided I would do a stand-up comedy routine. Honestly, I never tried to intentionally make people laugh, it is a gift from God. During the evening time each day leading up to the show, I worked on an approximate five minutes routine for the first time in my life. I never envisioned myself being a comedian, but why not showcase my talent since I wasn't shy about standing before a crowd? At the Christmas party, I stood before the staff fully prepared to bring unlimited laughter to the those present. As I expected, everyone laughed. Later that week, Bishop Owens called me and asked if I would perform that exact same routine for Greater Mt. Calvary Holy Church's New Year Eve service. I was elated and happily accepted. Instantly, my back started sweating because now I was going to be in front of a crowd of at least 1,500 people.

New Year's Eve, I got nervous. I was extremely nervous to the point of not only my back was drenched in sweat, but my hands felt clammy and my throat started to dry. *"Deep breaths, LaWan! You can do this! Just catch the eye of one person that's laughing and pretend that's the only person in the room. Walk the stage but look at the clock on the wall and not at the people. You got this girl,"* I coached myself! I performed my five minutes comedy routine, and not only did everyone laugh, but I received a standing ovation. I was so humble in that moment. People approached me after church service concluded asking for my business card and contact information so I could perform at their respective church, birthday party and the like. I didn't have any cards. Who knew a five-minute routine would garner a mass audience wanting to hear me again? I praise God for Bishop Owens and I am forever grateful. He saw a gift in me I that never saw in myself in this capacity. One that could be utilized in a positive way for the uplifting of people and bring healing to those in need. In the Bible, the book of Ecclesiastes 3rd chapter 4th verse talks about *"A time to weep, and a time to laugh..."* Indeed our gifts do make room for us.

Phone calls started to pour in soliciting me to perform comedy. God was truly opening doors that I'd never dreamt. After realizing teaching kindergarten children wasn't my special talent, I landed a job back in an office setting. Still unsure of what my exact purpose was, I knew working with children as a career was not it. My children remained students in CCA while I started my job as an Administrative Assistant and now a Christian Comedienne. After the Nova died, I purchased another used car from an auction. That car lasted as long as a cheap pair of shoes, so I then decided to step out on faith by purchasing a new car, with it came my very first car note.

After my divorce, I wanted a brand-new start in another city. I was starting to have disdain in my heart towards Washington, DC and felt like I needed to relocate to another zip code, area code, planet...just anywhere but here! I felt a fresh start was in order. I spoke with my mother's younger sister about my desire to relocate and she recommended Macon, Georgia which is where she lived, and offered to open her home to my children and me. Not bothering to pray about it, I gave my wonderful employer my two weeks' notice, my friends gave me a going away party, I sold and gave away my furniture, gave the rental office my 30 days' notice, then packed us up, with a little over $5,500 in my savings account and left the third week of June that year, after school ended.

Macon, Georgia was not for me. Oh boy, here I go again with making another horrible decision that appeared wonderful at the time it was decided. I never landed a solid job, despite my impressive resumé, superb interview skills, and winning personality. Between paying my car note, car insurance, groceries, paying living expenses in my aunt's house, clothes for the children and whatever else came up, my money in both checking and saving accounts depleted. Six months later I returned to the city that I was so in a rush to flee from. The Bible says; *"The steps of a good man has been ordered by the Lord."* God has a way of ordering our steps even when you think He's not doing the ordering. The good, the bad, the ugly, the indifferent, the mistakes, the choices...it all works together for the good of those who love God and are called according to His purpose.

    Dad happily opened his home to us, and we moved into the basement. The kids were enrolled into public school and starting over seemed to be harder than starting from nothing. The reason was because the battle was in my mind. I kept rehearsing my regrets and would not fully forgive myself. It took me YEARS to forgive me! Life happens! For the reader who may be beating yourself up over a decision that didn't quite pan out the way you envisioned, forgive you! Let it go. Cast all your cares upon God for He cares for you and He has already forgiven you.

    God truly blessed me prior to my drive north from Georgia to Washington, D.C. I had a phone interview with an incredible non-profit organization in Arlington, VA. When I met with them face-to-face, I was immediately hired as an Administrative Assistant. I met some amazing people, and as a result gained two more lifetime friends, Caletha Ellerbe and LaWan Croswell. (yep, she spells her first name just like mine. Lol) I worked there for a little over a year and then landed a job as a Project Coordinator for National District Attorney's Association (NDAA). A nonpartisan, prosecution organization. Their mission is to serve as the voice of America's prosecutors. I learned a lot at the company as I did with each company that I was previously employed. The best part about working at NDAA was traveling. Brent Berkley and Metria Hernandez, if you're reading this book, I love you both to pieces and you hold a special place in my heart! *wink* Amazing folks there!

It was time to return to school. Enough of hearing about the education accomplishments of others! No more being a hearer, but it was now time to be a doer. While working full time at NDAA and part-time as a weekend bouncer at Zanzibar nightclub, I enrolled in Spingarn Stay High School, which was night school. It's funny how things come full circle. Remember I attended in 1988, but those northeast girls kicked my butt and sent me packing. Here I was back in Spingarn but wiser and mature now. Courtney was in the 11th grade and here I, her mother, was in the "12th". I dropped out in the 12th grade so I wanted to finish what I started. I had taken the General Educational Development (GED) test but failed the Science and Mathematics sections of the test. Returning to high school was easier because I only needed to take four courses, and neither were Science and Mathematics.

Down through my career years, many companies sent me to a computer class here and there to brush up on skills or to learn new applications; great for adding to my resumé. But, going back to high school at 33 years of age was a different discipline. I was in the classroom with all kinds of personality types and all ages. Some mature, but most extremely immature. However, I remained focused and strongminded. I was in high school again. Again! This time with a second chance and a mindset not to repeat any past mistakes. God had done a tremendous work in me and He was on my team. I was not going to disappoint Him or myself. I had a vision and I saw myself going to prom, graduating at the top of my class and proudly walking across the stage wearing a cap and gown.

I was voted class president; such a prestigious honor and I represented the senior class well. At a class meeting we all voted unanimously to have a school prom, however the principal of the night school said we could not. Well, that didn't stop us from celebrating. I worked as a bouncer of a club so the senior class, those who were over the age of 21, all met at Zanzibar and we partied and deemed it our "Prom Night!"

Working two jobs, night school, raising teens & preteens was not easy at all. Projects at work had deadlines, traveling with my job was an obligation, homework assignments were expected to be done, then I still had to make time for my growing family. Thankfully three of my children were obedient and didn't cause trouble. Of course, no one is perfect, so I had challenges with the one that had my DNA coursing through his drug-free veins. During that time, I met and started dating my current husband, Kevin. Who was exceptionally patient when I told him very early in our courtship, "I may not have much time for you, because my life is full." He didn't seem to mind at all. Bless his loyal heart.

Graduation Day had arrived. I made it! And I graduated at the top of my class with a monetary award towards college books. That morning, celebrity make-up artist Mayvis Payne came to my home and created a masterpiece on this beautiful face. My children, my Daddy, Kevin, Amy, Earica Simmons, Yolanda Strother-Lawson, Sam Chandler, Darlene, nephews Troy and David were there to support! It was one of the happiest days of my adult life. Finally, I graduated! CONGRATULATIONS TO ME!!

I applied and got accepted into the University of the District of Columbia as a Criminal Justice major... With the vision in motion, my journey began.

THE JOURNEY CONTINUES...

Many who know me personally may have known my story or known some in part before I wrote it. There are hundreds of thousands who don't know me but could possibly find a part of them in my story. This was indeed a very hard book to write. To relive the painful parts of my past was the hardest. Once you get through something, it's over and behind you. But, when you must reach back and pull up that which you tried to bury in your subconscious, as you bring it to the front and face it, it's healing.

Volleying many stories in my brain trying to decide what will remain private and what I'll make public. God said, "Tell it. Be transparent." That was hard because I am very selective in what I share. How can a person heal or bring healing to others if they don't share their story?

I cried! Then I wiped my tears, only to grab another piece of tissue and cry again. Thank you, Lóreal, for creating waterproof mascara, because I did a good piece of crying for over two months while writing this book. At one point I kept trying to find places to write that I thought would allow me to write without shedding tears. Hotel rooms, Chipotle, Red Lobster, church, hospital visitors' room, customer waiting area at Ourisman car dealership...even took my laptop on a cruise with my husband and I. Just anywhere other than the quietness of my bedroom and home office. Not realizing it wasn't the places that caused an outpouring of tears, but the place in my heart that held hurt covered with life's blessings. The place in my heart that was still damaged. The place in my heart that I never dealt with fully. The place in my heart that wouldn't allow me to cry over my past. The place in my heart that said pull up your big girl panties and get over it. A lot was masked in pain. Smiling throughout, blocking out reminders of it. And even running from anything remotely familiar that'll trigger those painful parts. I even went as far as to avoid people who could possibly strike up a conversation with me about my history.

    One Wednesday morning I woke up and had this brilliant idea to take my laptop to the club and write there. Yep! I told my husband, "Kevin, I'm going to the VFW and taking my laptop so I can write." Always the ultimate supporter, he said, "that's a good idea, baby, do your thang." Smiling I said to myself, *"LaWan, there's no way you're going to cry in the club in front of all those people."*

It Ain't All Jokes!

Genius idea...or so I thought. I entered the club, speaking to kind patrons who knew me and others who didn't as I carefully peeled through the crowd heading for a table with an available chair. As godsend would have it, there was a partially empty table and an empty chair. Speaking to those at the table with a smile, I take a seat. Shimmying my shoulders to the song *Swag Surfin'* because DJ Rico was rocking on the one's and two's, I opened my laptop, opened my document, *It Ain't All Jokes!* and fixated on the bright screen. As a mother of four, I mastered the art of tuning things out, so the loud music, the dance floor, the twerkers, the men flirting loudly with the women, DJ Rico's robust voice belting through the mic, the contagious laughter around me were not a distraction, believe it or not. Opening my bottled water, courtesy of my lifetime friend Kenny, I picked up from chapter six where I left off. As I began to type about getting saved and believing that my daughter was the only thing I had left in the world and holding on to her was important for me April 16, 1990, I cried a river of tears January 2020. I cried cried! I cried hard! I tried to STOP myself from crying. I said to myself with tissue against my eyes, *"LaWan, get yourself together. You are in this club and people are watching you. Wipe your face and pull yourself together."* But the more I tried to toughen me up, the more I cried! Amazingly, no one bothered me. It was as if I was alone, just me and

God! Those tears were my release. It's okay now! Finally, it's okay. God was with me my entire life. He never left me neither did he forsake me. Although I felt abandoned, God was there all along. That's why I didn't die a pregnant homeless lady on the street. That's why He didn't allow the gunman to blow my brains out. That's why He didn't allow me to contract HIV/AIDS while I was bed hopping. That's why He didn't allow me to lose my mind when everything I tried to do failed.

When my grandmother died, I was shocked more than anything. She was a woman who prayed fervently and earnestly. I remember several occasions I would walk into her bedroom, spot her on her knees praying. It seemed I would always walk in just as she was in the middle of praying for me. She would say, "Lord, I wanna live to see LaWan change." After I got saved, she passed away a few months later. July 5, 1990 to be exact. God answered that prayer. She lived to see me change. Many prayers she prayed that He's still answering to this day. Her soul is in Heaven, but her prayers are still alive. I praise God that prayers don't expire because God is faithful.

It is my sincerest prayer that you were somehow healed, somehow forgave and perhaps you need to ask for forgiveness. You may be in an abusive situation or have a parent who neglected you in a way that you did not deserve. You may be currently experiencing domestic violence or in a relationship that's not healthy for you mentally, physically, or financially. Maybe you are unsure of what your purpose is; and you're still trying to find your way. Maybe your life is wonderful, but you've lost sight of how blessed you really are by taking family for granted. I hope this book has moved you in the direction of a better you.

I am LaWan Alexis Taylor Thompson. I am proud to say that I'm a wife, mother, grandmother, Christian comedienne, event host, caretaker of my father, Zumba instructor, entrepreneur, intercessor, mentor, motivational speaker, minister…oh, and a homeowner!! I am an abuse survivor and a thyroid cancer survivor. Although I've been diagnosed with arthritis, I believe God for the manifestation of total healing. Through this journey I found my purpose and passion. Although I've walked through the valley of the shadow of death, I came through unscathed, rebirthed and stronger than ever. I dare say, I don't look like what I've been through. My accomplishments are greater than my challenges and still God is adding so much favor and flavor to my existence. I am an overcomer with the courage to be all that God has created in me to be.

God is so amazingly wonderful, and I never would've thought in the beginning that I'd be at this place.

My failures turned into faith! My stress turned into shouts! My gloom turned into glory! My negatives turned into positives! My frowns turned into smiles! My weeping turned into joy! My anger turned into happiness! My unforgiveness turned into love!

I Corinthians 2:9 "Eye has not seen, nor ear heard, nor have entered into the heart of man, the things which God has prepared for them that love Him."

The best is yet to come...

And the journey continues...

GOD BLESS YOU ALL!!

It Ain't All Jokes!

DISCUSSION QUESTIONS

1. Do you think the violent culture and infestation of drugs in Washington, D.C. had any influence on the decisions that LaWan made?

2. Who was your favorite character and why?

3. What are your thoughts on drug addiction?

4. Did LaWan have the adequate support she needed while living with her mom?

5. What are your thoughts on forgiveness as it relates to LaWan and James' marriage?

6. How does Dad's love for LaWan correlates with your father's love for you?

7. How would you feel if you had to *Grow up Wanda*?

8. We know LaWan was raised in the 70's & 80's, which was a different era from today. What are some of the biggest differences and challenges that parents, and children face today?

9. What was your best part of the book? Why?

10. Are there any areas in your life that if you're transparent about them, can bring healing to others? If so, please share?

LaWan A. Taylor Thompson

To reach the author for questions, comments, or bookings:

- Instagram @lawantaylorthompson
- Facebook LaWan Taylor Thompson
- Email: <u>AuthorLaWan@yahoo.com</u>

LaWan A. Taylor Thompson

Made in the USA
Middletown, DE
27 July 2020